MW00675127

FORTY
WHACKS

By the same author:

Death in a Far Country

FORTY

WHACKS

A Brian Donodio Mystery

SHEILA MacGILL CALLAHAN

St. Martin's Press
New York

Library of Congress Cataloging-in-Publication Data

Callahan, Sheila MacGill.
     Forty whacks / Sheila MacGill Callahan.
         p.   cm.
     "A Thomas Dunne book."
     ISBN 0-312-11362-5
     1. Animal experimentation—Massachusetts—Fall River
—Fiction.   2. Research   institutes—Massachusetts—Fall
River—Fiction. 3. Fall River (Mass.)—Fiction. I. Title.
PS3563.A29825F67 1994
813'.54—dc20   94-3775
                                                      CIP

First Edition: November 1994

10 9 8 7 6 5 4 3 2 1

For the "Fall River Connection"
Patricia and Owen McGowan, and
Barbara and Bill O'Neil

Acknowledgments

Many thanks to Pat and Owen McGowan of Somerset, Massachusetts, and to Officer William O'Neil, Jr., of the Fall River Police Department and his wife, Barbara, for hospitality, information, and patience with endless questions. Accuracy is theirs, mistakes are mine. Dr. Ira Grossman, D.V.M. read my manuscript and offered invaluable advice as well as permission to use his clinic and his name. His sister is purely my invention. My husband, Leo Callahan, read and reread, commented and advised. I could not have managed without him.

Lizzie Borden took an axe
And gave her mother forty whacks;
When she saw what she had done
She gave her father forty-one!

—Anonymous

PROLOGUE

Liza Borden lay on her stomach on the blanket in that blissful state between waking and sleeping where one dreams at will and can steer the dream to a preferred ending. The April sun was surprisingly hot for so early in the season, but winter still lingered in the knife-edged wind and in the bare branches of the deciduous trees. Here and there, a flash of yellow or purple announced the arrival of early-blooming flowers and the faithful conifers flung their needled branches against the pale blue of the sky.

Through her dream, she could hear Joshua and the boys at the edge of the reservoir. The boys were excited about baiting their lines, happy with their father's full attention.

They had left Fall River long before daybreak and arrived at the Quabbin Reservoir, the great artificial lake that provides water to Boston and its surrounding communities, while the dew still shimmered on the grass. To the delight of the boys, they were early enough for a cookout breakfast of instant oatmeal, instant coffee, and instant cocoa.

It wasn't often that they could get away like this for a family outing, but today was Joshua's thirty-sixth birthday. When she asked him how he would like to celebrate, he had spoken wistfully of a family fishing outing to the Quabbin.

Liza had swallowed her own distaste at the idea and made all the arrangements. The boys were excused from school, a friend volunteered to mind Joshua's bookstore, and a colleague agreed to cover for her in case of any emergencies at the Delaney Institute, where she was resident veterinarian.

She stretched luxuriously and sat up to be sure that Nimrod, the younger boy, was safe. He stood between his father and brother, holding his toy fishing rod. His legs were planted apart and his attention was riveted on his bobbing float. Implicit in the set of his tiny shoulders was the message that today he was a man in a man's world. Liza sighed as she flopped back on the blanket and gazed up into the spring sky.

High over the reservoir, a dark shape soared in ascending spirals, riding the thermal updrafts. Liza grabbed her binoculars. The powerful lenses seemed to draw the bird so close that she could reach out and run her fingers over the snowy head and glossy wings. A bald eagle with the front set, yellow eyes, and strong hooked beak of a predator. Never mind the fishing, this had to be shared.

"Joshua, come here. Bring the boys," she called. "An eagle. A bald eagle this far south. Quickly, before she flies away."

For about an hour, they watched, taking turns with the binoculars, as the bird soared over the water. Several times, she swooped on some luckless fish and bore her victim triumphantly to her nest atop a tall white pine only about fifty yards away.

"I wish I could see into the nest," Liza muttered. "She must have chicks. I wonder if the conservation people know about this breeding pair?" She passed the glasses over to Nimrod, who was hopping up and down with impatience.

"Mama, she's caught a rabbit."

David grabbed the glasses away from his younger brother. "Let me see. . . . Yeah, it's a rabbit, a brown one with floppy ears. . . ." His voice trembled and he handed the glasses to his father. He looked green. "I don't want to watch a dumb old eagle. Let's go fishing."

Nimrod clutched at Joshua's pant leg. "Daddy, she won't eat the bunny, will she?"

Joshua was not a man to conceal hard truths from the young. "It's nature's way, son. She has to feed her own babies. David's right; we came here to go fishing. Let's go."

There was no sign of the male eagle. Odd, Liza thought as she followed the transport of the squealing rodent back to the tree, usually they take turns hunting and feeding the chicks. I hope nothing—

Suddenly there was the crack of a rifle. For a heartbeat, the great wings continued to fan the air, then her talons opened spasmodically to drop her prey and a red star blossomed on the white neck feathers.

Liza dropped the glasses. "Joshua," she screamed as she raced for the white pine.

The bird was dead. By the time Joshua and the boys came pounding up, Liza was climbing up to the nest.

Higher and higher, she climbed. In a detached corner of her mind, she blessed the anonymous bird watcher who had nailed slats to the tree trunk to provide a crude ladder to where the branches started, about thirty feet off the ground. Her heart pounded unpleasantly and she didn't dare look down.

"Liza," Joshua called from the ground, "come down. It's not safe. I'll go and call the state police. They'll have the proper equipment or know whom to call for help."

Kleel-kik-ik-ik-ik. She could hear the cackle of the chicks. She gestured impatiently and crouched on the limb just below the sturdy stick nest wedged like a platform between the highest branches, then raised herself cautiously so just her eyes cleared the edge.

Two nestlings, large and healthy-looking but only a couple of weeks out of the egg, crouched in the center of the platform. Liza ducked down and descended to the ground.

"Poachers! I'd like to kill them," she exploded when she reached the ground. "We have to call the police, though there's no chance that they'll catch the devil. He must have taken off as soon as he realized there were other people here. And I'll have to call Nina Buteo at the environmental office in Boston. I want to get those chicks for Delaney."

3

"Some birthday," Joshua remarked as he resigned himself to the inevitable. "What may we do to help?"

"Catch fish. We can use them to feed the chicks on the way back to Fall River."

After Joshua's birthday dinner, Liza came back for one last look at the chicks in their hastily constructed nest. It really was a blessing that they lived in what had been the gatehouse at the Delaney estate. It wasn't that she didn't trust the night man to follow her orders; it was just that she'd be happier if she checked on them once more before calling it a day. Her fear was that they would imprint on a human and be unable to mate when they were released into the wild. She corrected her thought: if they survived to be released into the wild.

She shrugged into her jacket and stepped outside. Joe, the night man, was pounding up the drive.

"Dr. Borden, thank God I caught you." Sweat poured down his face and his big hands were opening and closing as if he'd like to get them around someone's neck.

"What's the trouble? Did something happen to the eaglets?"

"No. It's the bears." His face was a curious gray under the blackness of his skin. "They're gone."

That was the start of the troubles.

"WE'RE DOING EVERYTHING we can. We've checked every lead and checked and cross-checked anyone connected with the institute. There's no trace of the missing bears and, as for the mutilated animals, the best theory seems to be some sort of religious cult. Of course, we do have some of that here in Fall River, but we have established no links between known cultic groups and Delaney's. All your staff and volunteers came up smelling like roses." Detective Umberto Suarez raised his hands helplessly and sat back in his chair to face the joint meeting of the staff and the board of directors. "I'm sorry, I just don't see how putting more people on the case will help. Captain McGuire here will bear me out. With my boss the chairperson of your board, you'd better believe that I'm giving this every effort."

"You'd better," Bill McGuire growled. He shifted his considerable bulk to a more comfortable position and ran a hand through his full head of white hair. "Thanks, Umberto. If there's nothing else anyone wants to know about your investigation, I'm sure you can be excused to get back to work."

Umberto Suarez was glad to get out into the fresh air. He was in a hell of a position, with his boss sitting on the board of the Delaney Institute and watching every move he made.

He had to walk on eggs. The old man was close to retirement and gossip around the Major Crime Unit was that he had his eye on the State House. Certainly it was true that he blew his stack at any detective who leaned too hard on citizens with money or political clout.

"Next on our agenda"—McGuire consulted his notes—"is our security arrangements. Do we need to increase them again?"

Liza raised her hand. "We already have committed a disproportionate part of our budget. If we keep spending at this rate, we won't have enough to pay our running expenses. What we've done so far seems to be working. We've had no new incidents for weeks."

"Nor are we getting any new animals. Word has spread and other facilities are afraid to trust us." McGuire's lips spread in a thin parody of a smile. "You all know the way we're set up. If we can't raise enough money to match the funding from the Delaney estate, the institute will be dissolved."

Liza looked around the finely proportioned room where the board met every Friday morning. It had been the library when this was a private house and still retained that function. Mrs Delaney's will had specified that the library remain intact and available to scholars. The shelves held one of the finest private collections in the country of books on natural history and the environmental sciences. Some, kept in locked, temperature-controlled cases, were rare fifteenth- and sixteenth-century herbals and botanicals. Stars of the collection were an 1827 edition of Audubon's *The Birds of America* and an 1854 signed copy of Thoreau's *Walden; or, Life in the Woods*.

The meetings used to be held monthly before the bears were stolen and other animals had been found killed or mutilated on the grounds. Now there seemed to be a new crisis every few days and the board was clearly splitting into factions.

In what Liza thought of as "her" group was Finbar O'Hanlon, who taught botany and horticulture at Bowhead College, and Abby Meyer, her best friend.

Verity Fletcher, the treasurer, and Caspar Lovelace, the attorney, seemed to take the same stance on issues and echoed each other automatically. Probably, Liza thought, because they've known each other forever and are both cut of the same Yankee cloth.

Pierre Bouchard, the secretary, struck her as a man with no firm convictions. He never joined in the discussions and always voted with McGuire.

As for McGuire, Liza didn't like him, but she had to admit he worked his butt off for the institute. The trouble was that he thought like a cop—his answer to everything was, "Increase security." And he might be right. If they'd had adequate security back in April, no one would have been able to steal the bears. Certainly, though, they could not afford to spend all their income on guards and electronic devices.

Discussion of further increasing security was tabled until the next meeting because Finbar O'Hanlon was practically dancing with impatience to be gone. "I'm sorry, everyone. I'm in the middle of an experiment and my seedlings may damp off. My heart is in Bowhead; my heart is not here. Liza darling, call me. I'd like you and that sweetie of a husband, Joshua, to come for dinner. Good-bye, all."

Bill McGuire followed his exit with narrowed eyes. "I don't know, there's something about that fellow . . ."

"Something very nice," Liza answered. She knew what McGuire reminded her of: a geriatric, overstuffed G.I. Joe doll.

Liza finished the draft of a letter to an old classmate at the National Forensics Laboratory in Ashland, Oregon, to bring him up to date on the latest developments at the institute. So far, there had been nothing practical that the lab could do, but it made her feel better to have someone at the U.S. Fish and Wildlife Service know what was going on.

She was tempted to call Joshua and cancel lunch at the bookstore, but he did enjoy it so—their quiet time together without the children. If she hurried, she'd be able to give the eaglets their noon feeding herself instead of leaving it to their keeper.

She worried about the chicks. It was high time for them to be hunting on their own, but they seemed perfectly content in their enclosure. Finbar O'Hanlon had devised a marvelous eagle hand puppet for their feeding, using their mother's own feathers and beak. Liza applauded the principle behind the device, but, as an observant Jew, she always felt it uncomfortably close to seething the kid in the mother's milk.

Feeding was through an expandable diaphragm like the lens of a camera. It was set into the base of a one-way mirror in the enclosure. With a little frisson of distaste, she fitted the puppet on her hand and grasped one of the strips of meat already laid out by the keeper. The chicks came pushing up, crowding eagerly to grab the food. It was over very quickly. After the first bite, they stiffened, twitched briefly, and died.

Detective Suarez had come and gone, taking the bodies of the eaglets and the remaining strips of meat for analysis. Before he arrived, Liza appropriated one of the strips for herself. She decided to send it to her friend at the National Forensics Lab for independent analysis. It was not exactly that she didn't trust the police; they just seemed so damned ineffectual.

As she plodded up the path to her office, she fought the temptation just to go home and deal with everything in the morning. Joshua would be there with the boys any minute. How long could she and Joshua go on like this? He had been full of concern when she called to cancel their lunch, but he let her know that he was getting fed up with the situation at Delaney. He had been after her to quit for some time and go into private practice. Why not? There was room for another vet in Fall River.

She took a deep breath and squared her shoulders. Private practice was a seductive dream, but where would they get the money to set up? Besides, something rotten was going on at the institute and she was going to get to the bottom of it. The first thing to do was to send the meat to her friend at the lab.

She was sure it was tainted with either nicotine or strychnine. But who would do that?

The envelope was squarely centered in the middle of her desk. She opened it and removed the folded paper. The words leapt up at her:

Bears
Cats/dogs/raccoons/squirrels/etc./
Eaglets
A dog named Mo-tze?
A cat named Solomon?
A vet named Liza Borden?

She didn't stop to think. She flew out of the office and down the path to the house.

Ira. She had to call her brother, Ira. Even more than Joshua, he would know what to do.

Nothing further happened. Hot summer melded into yellow autumn. No more mutilated animals, no more threats. The forensic lab confirmed that the chicks had been poisoned with strychnine. The police lab agreed. Liza started to hope that it was over, that some insane crank had either moved away, died, or gone into treatment. She started to relax.

Joshua had taken the boys to Heritage Park to ride the carousel and Liza was minding his bookstore. It was the night the store stayed open late, but no customers appeared. She poured herself a glass of white wine and sat down with a new mystery. Solomon, the Abyssinian cat, purred on her lap. Mo-tze, the beagle, pedaled his feet in a running dream at her feet. The phone rang.

"Liza? It's Abby." The voice sounded strange, muffled and far away.

"Abby? It doesn't sound like you. Where are you?"

"I'm here at the diamond in North Park. I have to see you right away."

"What on earth are you doing there? It's getting dark out. Josh isn't here and I can't leave the store."

The muffled voice rose. "It's an emergency. You can leave the store for a few minutes. Please."

"Abby, what's the matter?"

There was no answer but the click of the receiver.

North Park was only a five-minute walk away across Highland Avenue. Maybe she should call the police? No. Time enough for that when she found out what sort of fix Abby was in. She put a BACK SOON sign on the door and set out.

It wasn't really dark yet, but the park was deserted and shadowy. There were a couple of joggers in the distance. A cold wind whistled up the hill. Nothing moved.

"Abby," she called. There was no reply.

"Abby," she called again, "it's Liza. Where are you?"

Maybe she *should* call the cops. Come to think of it, was there a phone booth in North Park? Maybe someone was playing a joke. If so, it wasn't very funny. She took a few more reluctant steps onto the diamond. In the last few minutes, the sky had changed from twilight to dark.

The streetlights on Highland Avenue switched on. In their reflection, she made out a dark shape on the ground in the shadows near the dugout. She took a few more hesitant steps.

She inched closer.

She could hear her heart pounding in her ears. The dirt gritted under her feet, sifting over the tops of her shoes. She stubbed her toe on something hard and fell onto a thing that gave under her weight. Oh God! It was Abby. Abby, lying on her back. One side of her face was missing.

The thing Liza had tripped on poked into her shins, hurting. She reached to shift it. It was a bloody ax.

In the distance, she heard the sirens.

10

2

THE MEDIA DIDN'T just have a field day; they staged an olympiad. When the news broke that the police had arrested a woman named Liza Borden for the ax murder of Abby Meyer in Fall River, Massachusetts, their ecstasy knew no bounds. That the murder came about a hundred years after the original murder made their cups run over. The cherry on top was provided by the fact that the victim's name was Abby, the same as the original Lizzie Borden's stepmother.

ABC, NBC, and CBS sent camera crews. PBS got in on the action with grave documentaries about the original crime. The *National Enquirer* inquired LIZZIE REBORN? They came from London and Dublin, from Kuala Lumpur and Madagascar; here was an old-fashioned cause célèbre to take a weary world's eyes off Balkan wars, dishonest politicians, health care, and the Middle East.

Fall River responded with panache as Lizzie Borden buffs from all over the world came buzzing into town. Tours were organized, lectures presented. A special gala performance was mounted of Agnes de Mille's ballet the *Fall River Legend.* And, to the delight of all, the cash registers sang their happy song from morning until night. Hotels and motels were full, even the seedy joints on Route 6 and the fleabags on Bedford Street

11

where the trollops plied their trade. It was rumored that one lady of the evening scored so heavily that she was able to make a down payment on a 1760 Colonial with two riverfront acres in Somerset. She promptly joined the DAR and proved her descent from a Revolutionary War militiaman who had served his country well at the Battle of Bunker Hill. The DAR ladies were horrified, but what could they do?

The cause of all the hoopla languished in the Bristol County Jail and House of Correction in North Dartmouth. Her husband, Joshua Borden, was in despair. Her attorney, Rebecca Betancourt Delgado, Esq., had a motion for bail denied. Her brother, Ira Grossman, DVM, who had charged up to Fall River from his veterinary clinic in Far Rockaway, New York, cudgeled his brain.

"She's innocent," he repeated over and over like a mantra. "No motive. Abby Meyer was her best friend, for God's sake. What can we do?" It was then that he thought of his old friend and teacher Dr. Brian MacMorrough Donodio. There was no answer at Brian's number.

It was a perfect October afternoon—golden, mellow, with just a hint of underlying crispness. Brian MacMorrough Donodio settled back on the chaise in his arbor and gave himself up to a minor pleasure of the flesh. He felt he deserved it. Con and Deirdre's wedding was behind them and he was proud to have a son-in-law who was a detective sergeant in the NYPD and delighted that Deirdre had resigned her job with the INS, though he felt a stab of apprehension at whatever she might choose as a substitute occupation.

The first of the fallen leaves were raked and composted. The roses were tied up and pruned of dead wood. Hundreds of new bulbs awaited in serried ranks in the greenhouse. Next week, he would plant them in the double-dug beds that waited, as his aching back could attest. He pulled the ring tab on his can of beer. It yielded with a satisfying *pwoosht* and he tipped the amber contents into one of the frosted steins kept in the freezer for just such moments. Ahhh. The brew hit the back of his throat with a satisfying fizz. He picked up *The New York Times,* glanced at the front page, and did a double take.

"Maire," he yelled, "come here."

"Just a minute." His wife popped out of the kitchen door. "What's up?"

"Have you read today's *Times?*"

"I did the crossword. Before you say anything, I made a copy for you."

He thrust the paper under her nose. "Read that."

There was a minute's silence, then she looked at him with unbelieving eyes. "That's Liza Grossman, Ira's sister. She used to baby-sit for Deirdre. Ira was telling us at the wedding about how she married a fellow from Fall River named Borden and how everyone kidded her about it."

"The idea of Liza being an ax murderer is ridiculous." He pushed up from the chaise.

"Where are you going?"

"To call Ira."

"He's probably in Fall River."

"I'll call the clinic and find out."

She stooped to pick up the cat, Smith, who had followed her from the house. "I believe this cat is enceinte. She's getting a very round tummy."

"Right now, that's irrelevant."

"No it's not. If Ira's there, he'll be getting ready to go to Liza and he won't have time to talk to you. If he's already gone, his partner, Dr. Duffy, is going to be as busy as a dog with two tails and won't gossip on the phone."

Maire, as usual, made sense. "Let's take Smith to Rockaway."

Brian never drove if he could avoid it. He hated it, which made him a very bad driver. So it was Maire who turned into Queens Boulevard, the many-laned monster bisecting the largest New York City borough to the extreme detriment of pedestrians, both human and animal.

Brian shifted in the passenger seat. He was bored. God

13

knows, he had enough on his plate to keep five men occupied. Soon his classes would start again in the Irish Cultural Center, and he had a million and one family obligations, plus all the lecture dates resulting from the articles featuring Maire's interiors and his garden in various magazines. Could it be that his adventures of the past summer, when he had found himself a target in Ireland on Tara's Hill and fleeing for his life in the Donegal highlands, had awakened the genes handed down from some long-departed gallowglass ancestor? Mild-mannered retired history teacher becomes super-Celt?

His alter ego, the one that kept cutting him down to size, hopped out of his ear and perched on his left shoulder. (At least this was the way he always visualized it).

Face it, whispered the one on his shoulder, you want a little action.

"I abhor violence," he answered aloud.

"Of course you do, dear," Maire said. "It will take you a long time to put the whole sad business of Maureen Sullivan behind you. But that's all over."

The ghost of a snicker echoed in his ear: I don't hear the fat lady singing.

The traffic was light. Soon they had escaped the congestion of central Queens to skim along Crossbay Boulevard. Boredom or no, on a day like this it was good to be alive. Brian's mild depression evaporated between one breath and the next. By the time they pulled into the parking lot next to the veterinary clinic, he could scarcely contain his eagerness to find out exactly what was going on.

The small waiting room was crowded with resigned owners and apprehensive pets, rank with the mingled smells of pine disinfectant and urine. For years Brian had cultivated his nose until it almost (not quite) rivaled that of a nasally disadvantaged dog. Ira's clinic was not dirty, but he and his partner had a large practice and their congregation of dogs, cats, and other small creatures tended to generate a distinctive bouquet.

As Maire had predicted, Ira was nowhere in sight. His harassed partner was trying to deal with the animals as well as act as receptionist.

14

"Where's Ira?"

"I'm sorry, he's not here today. He has a family problem and had to go to Massachusetts. Our receptionist is sick and I'm trying to cope. I know Ira considers you a special client. If it's not an emergency, perhaps you'd prefer to come back when he returns," the young vet suggested hopefully.

"No. We've come quite a way; we'll wait." Maire glanced around the waiting room crowded with people and pooches. A steady snarl was emanating from Smith in the carrier. "Why don't I wait outside with her until you're ready. I think she's unhappy."

Brian followed *All Creatures Great and Small* devotedly on PBS. "Why don't I come inside and give you a hand? I've done it before with Ira."

"Great." Dr. Duffy ushered him in and handed him a green smock. "Put that on. You can hold the patients while I do my dirty deeds. It looks unprofessional to ask the patients to hold their own animals. He stuck his head into the waiting room. "Mr. Campbell, I'll take Max now."

Max looked to be a cross between a St. Bernard and a woolly mastodon. When Brian reached for his collar, he made noises expressive of his opinion of Brian's ancestry and raised his lip on one side to flash a two-inch fang.

"Just pop him up on the table." Jim Duffy's voice emerged from the depths of a cupboard where he was assembling several disgusting instruments.

Brian eyed Max warily. Max reflashed his denture. "You do it, Jim. I don't think he likes me very much."

Jim glanced a comprehensive veterinary glance. "I see you might feel a little intimidated, but actually there's nothing to it." He advanced on Max, who promptly flashed the fang. "Er . . . maybe we'd better have the owner in. Just stick your head out and call Mr. Campbell."

The arrival of Mr. Campbell made both of them feel like idiots. Campbell was a spruce, dapper man about Brian's age but a good head shorter. He shook his head.

"I never have any trouble with him. I just can't understand

15

why people are so intimidated." He patted the examining table, then snapped his fingers. "Max! Up!"

Max proved that Campbell was not a liar. He jumped onto the examining table and sat without a quiver, only voicing a tiny whimper when the needles popped in.

Max's place was taken by a Labrador pup that posed no problem except exciting a strong desire to scoop up the little guy and take him, or one like him, home. Brian hardened his heart. He knew that puppies have to be walked regardless of weather and that their delight was the burial of bones in flower beds. They chewed shoes and peed on rugs. They chased cats and had to be taught the error of their ways. He knew he was going to break down and adopt one. But today he had Liza on his mind.

Jim Duffy kept darting glances at him. Brian could tell that he was dying for a good gossip but thought it would look unprofessional. Well, he was right: It would. He decided to nudge him a little.

"You mentioned that Ira was called away by a family problem?"

"Have you ever met his sister?"

"Liza? I've known her since she was a kid with braces. Ira and she were both my students at Prendergast. She used to baby-sit for our younger daughter." He was about to add that the charges against her were ridiculous, then changed his mind. He might get more information out of Jim if he played dumb.

Duffy's eyes were dancing with the glee of someone not personally involved who is about to drop a bombshell. "Have you been reading about the Lizzie Borden murder in Fall River?"

"Along with the rest of the world, yes. You're not saying that Lizzie Borden is Liza Grossman? That's ridiculous!"

"I guess it doesn't seem too ridiculous to Ira and Liza."

Smith was, indeed, pregnant. On the way home, Brian filled Maire in on all he had gleaned from Jim Duffy.

16

"I've got to go to Fall River."

"What do you mean, 'got to'? Has anyone asked you?"

"No. But maybe I can help."

A red flush mounted on Maire's neck. "Like the last time?"

Brian shifted defensively in the passenger seat. "I found out who murdered Maureen, didn't I?"

"And nearly got killed in the process. Almost made me a widow. Nearly ruined Deirdre and Con's wedding."

"I admit things got a little out of hand. But this time, it would be entirely different."

"Different? How?" She turned off to Woodside and home. "First, how do you *know* Liza Grossman is innocent? The police arrested her standing over that poor woman's body with the bloody ax in her hands. Second, if she is innocent, there's someone running round loose in Fall River who is a particularly vicious murderer and a neat hand with a hatchet." She played her trump card: "If I hear another word, I'll tell Con and Deirdre on you. Have you forgotten that we're going to their house for dinner tomorrow night?" She pulled into the driveway, killed the engine, and stormed into the house.

As always, Brian paused to survey their domain. The garden had been manicured within an inch of its life for Con and Deirdre's wedding reception. The summer blooms were mostly gone, but fall flowers rioted in their darker, richer tones—freesia, chrysanthemums of all sizes and colors, daylilies, sedum, and monkshood. He could not see the vegetable patch and the fruit trees from the street, but he knew they were bountiful with brussels sprouts, kale, pumpkins, squash, late tomatoes, apples, and pears. The dwarf burning bush beside the doorway flaunted its crimson leaves.

How right he and Maire had been to buy this place and how it had repaid their loving restoration. They were convinced that the oldest part of the house predated the 1661 Bowne House in Flushing, but they kept their suspicions secret from historical societies and landmark commissions.

When they bought the place after World War II, it was a botched-up horror of jerry-built additions and sagging, peeling siding. The space was handy when two sons and two daughters followed in quick succession. As each left home, the house got smaller as the accretions were stripped away.

Now the original Dutch farmhouse with one added Federal wing stood in his lush garden, and Maire had realized her talent in researching the restoration.

Maire. Right now she was in a snit, but she'd get over it. After forty years of marriage, he still smiled at the thought of her. Forty years and he could honestly say he had never been bored or looked to greener fields. Sure, they had disagreements. But how many other couples of their vintage still went to bed at night (and other times) with a sense of anticipation? He opened the door.

The wide central hall stretched the length of the house in the old Dutch fashion, enfolding him with mingled scents of wax, lavender, and spaghetti sauce from Maire's kitchen. It had been simmering gently all the time they were in the wilds of Rockaway. Maire stood in the hallway, the light of battle still strong in her eyes.

He advanced with outstretched arms. "Peace. Do we have time for a preprandial aperitif?"

"Why not? I'll have my usual." She switched on the lights in the living room and drew the curtains against the gathering dusk.

Brian returned from the kitchen. "Here we are, one vodka and cranberry for you, two fingers of Glenties single malt for me."

They both started to speak at once, then courteously deferred to the other. Perhaps there is a divine serendipity, or it may just be the ingrained American custom of ladies first. Maire went first.

"You'll never guess what came in the mail while we were out."

"Not unless you tell me."

"An invitation from the Blessington Museum in Kansas City. They want me to design a series of exhibition rooms." Her blue eyes were snapping with excitement and her cheeks glowed. "I have to call tomorrow and speak to a Mr. Knabe; he's the curator for their collection of Americana."

She got up and spun around the room like a five-foot top. "It's just what I need to finally get over the wedding. And the Blessington! It's one of the most prestigious museums in the Midwest! What do you think?"

"Of course you have to go; it's a wonderful offer." And I can go to Fall River, he thought. "When do they want you?"

"They'd like me to fly out on Monday for a conference, and I'll be gone for about a week organizing things. Then, once it's organized, I'll fly out every week for a couple of days. And they're offering me a free hand, a generous budget, and a consulting fee that will grow hair on your head, never mind our accountant's."

Hair was a sore subject. Brian reached up and smoothed his sparse locks self-consciously.

Her lips pursed and a calculating gleam appeared in her eyes. "At least that's what the letter implied. I'll probably find all sorts of ifs and whereases when I actually get there. You're sure you don't mind?"

"Mind? Why should I mind? I think it's great, and when the exhibit opens, I'll be right there with my bald pate too big for my hat."

The long case clock in the hall was striking two when Brian came wide awake with a name clutched firmly in his mind. Dennis Duque was in Fall River. Dennis and he had been best buddies fifty-five years ago at St. Camillus parochial school in Rockaway Park and they had seen a lot of each other until Dennis went to Canada to become a Sulpician priest. He had officiated at Maire's and his wedding. After that, they'd drifted apart, but a few years ago he'd heard that Dennis was stationed at St. Fiacre's parish in Fall River. It was time to renew an old friendship. He turned on his side and fell into a deep sleep.

3

As was his wont, Brian rose early the next morning to attack his garden while the bird was on the wing and the snail on the thorn. There was work to be done; there were thoughts to be thought and plans to be laid.

He surveyed his double-dug beds as an artist surveys a virgin canvas and decided on a random mixed effect for the coming spring instead of carefully planned contrasting banks of color. To this end, he tossed handfuls of mixed bulbs, dibbling them in wherever they happened to land.

Dibbling is a mindless occupation. His thoughts revolved around Liza Grossman, aka Borden. Guilt was an unacceptable option. The gentle, brilliant girl he'd known years ago could no more have grown into an ax murderer than her brother, Ira.

He realized he was spinning his wheels. The thing to do was try to call Ira at the number Jim Duffy had given him. He dug in the last bulb and hotfooted it to the kitchen, coffee, and a phone.

Maire was up, coffee brewed, popovers popped, and tumblers of fresh-squeezed orange juice waiting on blue linen place mats. He spied an omelette.

"A vision, an ocular poem." He kissed her enthusiastically. "What gets you up so early?"

20

"Things," she answered vaguely.

"What sort of things?"

"I have to find some material I need to refer to when I call Mr. Knabe at the Blessington. And I want to sort out some of Deirdre's things. We can take them to her this evening when we go for dinner. And"—she skewered him with an accusative eye—"I'm going to pack the things you'll need in Fall River."

He collapsed in his chair. "Am I that transparent?"

"Not to most people, but to me, yes. Now, hurry up and eat; we have work to do. By the way, I called Ira's wife. She drove up to Fall River with him to bring Liza and Joshua's two boys back to the city. She gave me the number where you can reach Ira."

"Hold your tongue. Are you trying to tell me that maybe he doesn't want me?" Even as he spoke, he was punching in the numbers. "Hello, this is Brian Donodio. May I speak to Dr. Grossman? . . . No, I'm an old friend. If you'll just tell him I'm on the line, calling from New York . . . No, I am *not* a reporter. . . . To whom am I speaking? . . . Well, Ms. Betancourt Delgado, would you be kind enough to give him a message that I called and have him call me back. . . . Not necessary, he knows my number." He slammed down the receiver. "Well, that puts me in my place."

"Come and eat your breakfast before it gets cold. He'll call back."

"Let's see if we can catch anything new about Liza on TV." Brian wiped his mouth and folded his napkin before pushing back from the table. They had spent the previous evening channel hopping.

"Nothing new. I already checked." Maire looked up from loading the dishwasher. "Wait until I make my call to the Blessington and get out the stuff for Deirdre. Then, if Ira hasn't called, we can go to Rockaway and visit Rivka Grossman. She can tell you everything and you can try Ira again from there."

"How are Liza's kids taking it? Did she say?"

"She said Nimrod, the four-year-old, is too young to really understand, but he does sense that something is terribly wrong. The elder boy, David, woke up screaming last night. It's only to be expected."

"Maybe I might . . ." Brian started. Whatever he might do was never revealed. The phone rang, it was Ira.

4

After Brian accompanied Maire to La Guardia Airport for her flight to Kansas City, he gritted his teeth and got behind the wheel to make his own way to Fall River.

It had been years since he had undertaken such a drive on his own. He eyed the bumper-to-bumper lines on the Grand Central Parkway and brooded on an advertisement in *House & Garden* he had found hilarious when he read it to Maire months ago. It touted (maybe *pimped* would be a better word) Nissan's new luxury model, misspelled as Infiniti: "It's not a car. It's an aphrodisiac." Well, his '88 Chevy was a lot of things, but that was one claim it could never make.

But those who learn to drive in New York City traffic cut their teeth in a stern school and their training stays in place. As time passed with no major disasters, the vise gripping his back and neck muscles gradually relaxed. He started to enjoy himself.

When Ira and he had finally spoken, he had deemed it good strategy not to seem too eager. In fact, he had put up a show of modest self-deprecation and allowed himself to be wooed.

"My dear fellow," he had protested, "I'm not a detective. I got into that business in Ireland wholly by accident and was lucky to get out with my skin. How could I possibly help you?"

In the end, they had agreed that he be introduced as a consultant to the family, a title that was conveniently vague. They had also agreed that he should arrive in Fall River unannounced.

The dinner at Deirdre and Con's house in Chelsea had gone well. After admiring the transformation wrought by Maire and Deirdre on the two upper floors of the brownstone they shared with Con's widowed mother and sister, the conversation turned to plans for the future.

Newlyweds tend to be self-centered. It's nature's way. It was easy for Brian to mention vaguely a trip to New England and have it accepted instead of dissected. At any rate, the big news belonged to Maire, with her dream assignment at the Blessington. With any luck at all, he would be in and out of Fall River before Con and Deirdre realized he was mixed up in another murder case.

No need to chance his arm on the Connecticut Turnpike. He meandered along on the secondary roads through the small towns and villages on the Connecticut shore. It was only a little north of the city, but already a dipping jet stream had delivered the first frost and the oaks and maples blazed with the shouting reds of fall.

At New Haven, he paused to make a phone call to an old acquaintance whom he hoped to enlist in Liza's cadre. Professor (emeritus/Yale) Philander Dobbs had an international reputation among the small percentage of the earth's billions who knew about the demise of *Hispaniolan hexolobodia* and *Puerto Rican caviomorphs*. In other words, Dobbs was a zoologist specializing in endangered and extinct Caribbean species. Though the Delaney Institute would not play host to any creatures from his particular specialty, they would hardly refuse to receive a scientist of his eminence. He could learn a lot. He was also a devoted and avid gardener. He was at home and delighted to invite Brian to lunch.

This was the first time Brian had ever been a guest in Professor Dobbs's home. Until now, their friendship had been strictly horticultural, nurtured at meetings, exhibits, and by correspondence. A couple of wrong turnings delayed him about fifteen minutes. He gazed openmouthed.

Set foursquare in the middle of about three acres of mature garden was a pillared, lavishly porticoed house-size clone of the Treasury Building in Washington.

Dobbs must have been watching. The door opened and out he came. "Here you are, my dear fellow. Most get lost and turn up hours late." He never forgot that he had been a Rhodes scholar. His accent was a strange mixture of flat Yankee and plummy Brit.

Brian was not to be outdone by any descendant of the Pilgrim Fathers. He slapped his old Chevy with affection. "In the words of Browning, 'He walked his managed mule without a tittup.' Good to see you, Dobbs. Quite a place. Did Robert Mills design it as a Washington spin-off?"

"Right first try. I'm impressed. Emily is waiting and lunch is ready. Unfortunately, it's a bit too brisk to eat on the terrace." He stood aside to let Brian precede him.

The interior was as Brian expected. Chill with marble, stiff with uncomfortable, ornate furniture. On the walls, ancestors in gilded frames peered down their long Yankee noses.

Just the sight of them made Brian sniff up his long Roman nose. He detected a touch of damp in the foundation and dry rot in the beams; the cold, dead smell that marble gets in an interior where the sun cannot warm it. The smell of decay was very faint. Those living in the house would not even notice. He should warn Dobbs to have it checked.

His host waved a dismissive hand. "Terrible place, totally unlivable. Nothing we can do about it. Guided tours, National Register, historic significance, the children—all that sort of twaddle." He paused before an inconspicuous door in the back of the hall. "We built a small addition onto the back. This is where we live." He opened the door and they stepped into another world.

Sunlight flooding through the rear wall of glass glanced off a red tile floor covered with woven grass and sisal mats. Wicker chairs with fat chintz cushions, each flanked with its own handy table, clustered informally around a blue-tiled central fountain. Plants were everywhere. There was too much everywhere. One end of the solarium was a mini–rain forest with a mini–weather system to keep it moist. The trouble was, it kept everything else moist, as well. No wonder there was a smell of damp in the main house.

Emily was a surprise. Brian had expected a silver-haired lady with pearls. In fact, she was at least twenty years younger than Dobbs and powerfully built. Her blue-black hair drew smoothly back into a no-nonsense bun. He sniffed, but she smelled of nothing more exotic than lavender soap and . . . could it be that those raven tresses owed more to artifice than to Mother Nature? She was clearly mistress of the house, but she wore no wedding ring. Brian thought, Philander, you old devil, you have a significant other. She came forward with outstretched hand.

"Dr. Donodio, it's a pleasure. I'm Emily deRosa."

"Then you are my *paisana*. It's a pleasure to meet you, Ms. deRosa."

"Dr. deRosa," Professor Dobbs corrected.

"Please, call me Emily."

They ate lunch by the fountain, a toothsome salad of yellow beets and radicchio garnished with calendula flowers. It was served with a mild, slightly fruity white wine and fresh-baked sourdough rolls. Dessert was a compote dish of fresh raspberries with cream, served along with Italian coffee strong enough to hold a spoon erect. The three eaters paid the food the compliment of silent pleasure.

Brian wiped his mouth. "Magnificent. Was it your work, Emily?"

"Guilty. But I stole the recipe for the salad from Martha Stewart's *Gardening Month by Month*. Do you know it?"

"I do indeed. But I'm afraid I skipped the cookery chapters. I'll point them out to Maire when I next see her. She's the cook in our house."

A light of feminist combat glowed in Emily's eyes. Philander moved quickly to forestall her. "What is your wife up to lately? I've never had the pleasure, but I've heard she's very highly considered in her field."

26

"You see before you a grass widower. Maire is away for a week in Kansas City organizing an exhibit for the Blessington."

Emily's eyes lighted up. "Are you married to *the* Maire Donodio? The interior designer?"

"Now that you mention it, yes."

"I wish I'd known." She looked at Dobbs accusingly. "Why didn't you tell me who he was?"

"I did. I told you Brian Donodio was coming."

"But not who his wife is. We were just talking about her at work the other day." She laid her hand on Brian's arm. "I'm an editor at the university press. We'd be very interested in talking to Mrs. Donodio about doing a book for us. I can't tell you what a piece of luck it is having you here today."

It was a personal historic moment for Brian. For the first time, his worth was measured by the fact that he was Mr. Maire Donodio, and he didn't like the feeling—damn it, he'd accomplished a few things in his sixty-five years. He felt castrated. Was this how women felt all the time? Emily grinned knowingly as she waited for his reply.

"You would have to contact Maire about it; she and I are quite independent professionally." He grinned back. "Of course I'll tell her that I met you and the impression I gained."

"A good one, I hope." He didn't rise to the bait. "I have to get back to my office for a meeting, but I do have time to show you my own modest effort." She led them out into the garden, where she cultivated a kitchen garden she called her *potagerie*. "I did graduate work in Paris and was impressed by the way the French coax vegetables out of every tiny plot."

Brian nodded. "Nothing like the French."

"I'm sorry I can't stay for the whole afternoon," she reiterated. "I'll write very soon to Mrs. Donodio. I hope you're still here when I get home."

After the round of the gardens and the greenhouse, Philander and Brian settled in the fountain room. Brian believed that those who were not against him were for him. He went straight to the point.

"Dobbs, I have a three-pipe problem and I've come to you for help."

"Speak on, Macduff. Are you mixed up in another thing like last summer? I read about it in the *Times.*"

"I don't know what I'm mixed up in as yet. Let me lay it out for you, as the children would say."

"Must you? Can't you just tell me in the Queen's English?"

"You know about the Lizzie Borden brouhaha in Fall River?"

"My dear fellow! Every newspaper, radio, and television program has been pounding it into our ears ad nauseam. You don't mean to tell me that's what brings you here?"

"In a nutshell, yes. Liza Borden and her brother, Ira, were students of mine years ago at the Prendergast School. Ira is now our vet and a very dear friend. Liza became a vet as well and moved to Fall River after she married a chap named Borden."

"This sounds like a long story. Hold on for a moment while I get something to ease the telling. What are you drinking?"

"Two fingers of Glenties single malt, if you have it."

"Would you settle for Laphroaig?"

"Need you ask?"

"I'll only be a minute." Dobbs heaved to his feet and disappeared into another room.

Left to himself, Brian stretched to his full length in the chair. He thought, why am I doing this? He remembered the bullet that had nearly ended his life on Tara's Hill, the thug who beat him up in Dublin, and sheer terror turning his bowels to water in the Donegal highlands. He could be at home getting a start on the book he had been talking about writing for years on Suger of Saint-Denis.

But here he was, a damn-fool retired teacher, scared to death but feeling alive down to his very toenails. That was what hooked him, not a thirst for justice. He felt alive, vital, of use. It was his way of fighting the senior-citizen syndrome.

Dobbs interrupted his musings with a glass of the best. "Here's to crime. Go on with the story."

"You've read the newspaper reports. What I'm telling you

28

comes from Liza's brother and sister-in-law. Liza is the resident vet at a place called the Delaney Institute in Fall River. They're doing work on endangered species. She lives with her husband and two sons in what was the gate lodge on the Delaney estate. The murder victim, Abby Meyer, was on the governing board of the institute."

Dobbs stirred in his chair. "I know the work of the Delaney outfit. They have a fine facility and have done good things, but there have been rumors lately that they've been having problems."

"That's putting it mildly. Ira tells me that it started last spring when a bear and her two cubs disappeared. No explanation—they just vanished from the enclosure one night."

"Nobody saw anything? A full-grown bear isn't easy to steal inconspicuously."

"Security was light. Just a night watchman who seems to have spent most of his time watching old movies on TV. They'd never had any trouble. Then mutilated animals started showing up on the grounds—nothing endangered, just stray dogs and cats, rabbits, a couple of raccoons, a doe and her fawn."

Dobbs stirred to interrupt the flow, but Brian was in full flight. The voice that had enthralled generations of students and interested them in the Punic Wars rolled on.

"Then there were the eagles."

"Eagles?"

"Last April, Liza rescued two unfledged chicks when their mother was shot by a poacher at the Quabbin Reservoir. She was raising them, feeding them with an eagle puppet covered with the feathers of their dead mother and using their mother's beak to hold the food."

Dobbs grimaced. "Talk about seething a kid in his mother's milk."

"Definitely not kosher, but it was effective. The babies thrived and the object was achieved."

"Damn clever, actually. If they'd impressed on a human, they'd never have been able to mate."

"A while back, Liza went to feed them. The meat was all

29

cut and waiting for her. Both youngsters grabbed the food, shuddered a couple of times, and fell over dead. When Liza got back to her office, there was a note on her desk saying the same thing could happen to her dog, her cat, and herself."

"So someone's out to get Liza?"

"Or someone's out to ruin the Delaney Institute and thinks it can best be done through discrediting Liza, and what is more discreditable than a murder charge? You're a specialist in the endangered-species trade. Any ideas?"

"The thing that leaps to mind is her name. I could see that a crazy might not be able to resist having a second Lizzie Borden murder in Fall River. Is she connected to the original Borden family?"

"No, Liza is Jewish and so is her husband. I don't know the whole story. Her brother told me that the family name is really Brodsky and he'd tell me all about it sometime."

"Fall River," Dobbs mused. "Now, who do I know around there? There's a terrible little college just between Fall River and New Bedford—Bowhead College. It's one of those places that latched onto the GI bill and got too big for its britches. Started back in whaling days as a finishing school for young ladies whose families were too high up for the public schools and too low for the fancy places in Boston and New York."

"How can Bowhead College help?"

"It could provide a reason for your presence in the area. By the way, you'll be very welcome if you would like to stay with us tonight and continue your journey in the morning. We have plenty of room, and Emily would be delighted."

Brian accepted with pleasure.

"Now, about Bowhead. I know the president, chap called Leander Seward. He's a Yale man and we were in the same class back in prehistoric times. Poor Lee was never much good at anything, no self-confidence. Thought he was inferior to his classmates. As a result, he overcompensated and tried to be holier than the Pope, if you know what I mean. His life ambition was a professorship at Yale, but he had to settle for Bowhead."

"You don't make him sound like a boon companion."

"The man's an ass. However, he did one thing properly. Thirty years ago, he hired a chap who rejoices in the name of Finbar Duane O'Hanlon. Have you heard of him?"

"Sure. Didn't he write *Cover Your Ground* and *The Death You Pick May Be Your Own?*"

"That's the fellow. He's about as big as a minute, but he's a tough, feisty Irishman. I'm practically positive that he lives in Fall River. I manage to get up to Bowhead a couple of times a year to see what new cultivars he has up his sleeve. His department is about the only thing Bowhead has going for it. I think it's about time I paid him a visit."

"You don't mean . . ."

"Sure I do. You just picked up a Watson. Don't forget, I'm an endangered-species person and your Liza strikes me as very endangered."

"I hadn't forgotten. Why do you think I'm looking so smug?"

"Entrapment? Pat yourself on the back. It worked."

5

BRIAN SAT BACK and surveyed his host. The years had not been kind to Dennis Duque. Somewhere buried in that defeated mountain of fat had to be the quicksilver, agile little boy from St. Camillus. The friend who shared the long, hot, idle days of remembered summers when they explored the salt marshes and coves of Jamaica Bay. And where was the soulful-eyed teenager who had left a trail of broken hearts from Breezy Point to Far Rockaway when he suddenly announced that he was going to be a priest?

Well, God bless him. When so many left the priesthood in the turmoil following the sixties and the Second Vatican Council, he'd remained true.

"It's been a long time, Dennis."

"Too long. And a lot of water under the bridge."

"Surprised?"

"Not the word. I practically shat bricks when you called."

"You always did have a gift for the telling phrase and your grammar is impeccable. How does one decline the verb *to shit? Shit, shat, shot?*" Brian looked around the room. Both the church and the rectory were bastardized Bauhaus, typical of the excrescences built in the *aggiornamento* enthusiasm.

"What brings you to Fall River? Surely not to visit me after, what is it, nearly forty years? I haven't clapped eyes on you since I officiated at your wedding."

Brian had prepared his story, but he was a lousy liar. This was his old pal—and bodies may change, but people don't. Besides, Dennis was a priest and had probably heard stranger tales than his. He leveled with him.

As Dennis listened, the years seemed to fall away and the old devil-may-care light gleamed in his eyes. "That's quite a story. Of course, the Delaney Institute has been big news here since last April when the troubles started. By all accounts, the police are, as they say, baffled. What may I do to help?"

"I'm just feeling my way. Have you heard any rumors? Things not reported in the papers?"

"I know Josh Borden, of course. He runs the best book-store in Fall River. It's one of my favorite places."

"I know about the store; Ira told me. I wouldn't think it would be open with all that's going on."

Dennis heaved his bulk out of the chair. "Why don't we take a ride around town so you can orient yourself? I'll be your tour guide. We'll go by the bookstore and out to Delaney's, then stop for lunch in a little Ukranian place down on Globe Street where they serve the best kielbasa and pierogies in town. Let's go."

"Just like that?" Brian's eyebrows rose. "Aren't you sup-posed to be here at the rectory?"

"Priests have a lot of free time these days, or haven't you heard? The parish council, the secretary, and the housekeeper run the parish; the sisters and the lay teachers run the school. Me, I eat and get fatter, except on Sundays, when they trot me out to work the magic." There was a world of bitterness in his voice.

"But surely . . ."

"It's the way of the world, Brian. You and I are going the way of the dinosaur. Come on, I'll show you my takeoff on Father Dowling."

"Make it Father Brown and you're on."

"You mean you'd rather be Flambeau than Sister Stepha-nie?"

"At the risk of being labeled a chauvinist, yes." Brian grabbed his coat. "Dennis, it is *so* good to see you. Why did we ever lose touch?"

He did not answer. "Your car or mine?"

"Let's take mine. You be navigator."

The schoolyard next to the church was full of children. Brian paused for a moment to watch a group of little girls playing jump rope. They were chanting a skipping rhyme. His scalp contracted as he listened.

> *Liza Borden took an axe.*
> *She gave poor Abby forty whacks.*
> *Abby Meyer gave a yell.*
> *Liza Borden went to hell.*
> *One, two, three . . . red hot pepper*

"Is there much of that going on?"

Dennis shrugged. "What do you expect? Even if she's judged not guilty, she'll have to get out of Fall River.

"Not if we find out who really did it."

"I've given instructions to the faculty to clamp down on that sort of thing and give lessons on 'innocent until proven guilty,' but kids will be kids. Come on, there's nothing you can do about it."

St. Fiacre's was on the south side of the city. Brian followed directions to the north side and the higher ground overlooking the water. They emerged from the doldrums of Main Street to ride past the bus terminal and a small mall typical of the last twenty years of frantic urban renewal.

Dennis called his attention to a gaunt nineteenth-century Greek Revival house on Second Street with a printing press occupying an annex added to the ground floor.

"See that place over there? That's the old Borden house, where Lizzie allegedly 'took an axe and gave her mother forty whacks.' "

"Allegedly?"

"Well, she was acquitted. Personally, I always thought her

34

sister, Emma, was the guilty party. I guess it's all academic now."

"And she's comparing notes with Jack the Ripper and they're laughing up a storm. Where do I go now?"

"I'll tell you when to turn. This section is called the Highlands. Wealthy mill owners caught the breeze and good air while the masses sweltered or froze below. Of course that was before the textile industry moved south and overseas. Most of the great mansions have been torn down and the big Victorian houses are broken up into apartments."

"And around St. Fiacre?"

"The three-deckers? They're known locally as 'tenements' and the one-family houses are 'cottages.' A building has to be pretty spiffy to get called a house. Now, hang a left at the next corner and down the hill one block to that little red cottage on the corner."

Josh Borden's bookstore was nestled on a tiny lot under a huge oak. Ivy spread up the walls of the house and the minuscule brick walk was flanked by dark red and white chrysanthemums. The sign hanging from a wrought-iron bracket read, BORDEN'S BOOKS, and in smaller letters underneath, BROWSERS WELCOME, PLEASE RING BELL. Not expecting a response, they rang the bell.

A dark-haired man in his late thirties answered the door. He was six feet or a shade less and had thinning curly hair. Horn-rims magnified nearsighted red-rimmed eyes. He sported a full beard and his head was crowned with the yarmulke of an observant Jew.

"Father Duque, I'm sorry, but I'm really not open today. I'm sure you understand. I just came over here to try to escape from the media vultures."

Before Dennis could explain, Ira Grossman rushed out and grabbed Brian in a bear hug. "Brian, thank God you've arrived. Joshua, this is the Dr. Donodio I was telling you about. Come in; come in."

The tiny entry led directly to a perilous unbanistered, twisting staircase to the upper floor. On either side, doors led into two fair-sized rooms lined floor to ceiling with books. The only breaks were for windows in the front and, on one wall, a blazing open fireplace. A middle-aged beagle lounged on the hearth with a magnificent Abyssinian cat cuddled between his paws.

"Meet Mo-tze the dog and Solomon the cat."

Brian crouched down to exchange courtesies. "Is that Matzoth for Passover or Mo-tze the philosopher?"

"The philosopher, but we like the pun." Joshua smiled sadly. "Liza named him. You know, you're the first person who caught it."

Joshua's remark put the seal on Brian's surety of Liza's innocence. No one who could make outrageous bilingual puns could be an ax murderess. He sniffed the good odor of paper, glue, and ink from the new books, overlaid by the gentle, but no less pleasant, sweet, sharp tang of older, secondhand volumes. This was a grand place.

He liked the gentle scholarly man peering through his thick lenses. Ira had told him that the little store hardly made expenses. Without Liza's earnings as a vet, they'd have real trouble meeting the mortgage and paying the fees at the private nursery school for the younger boy. The elder boy was in third grade in public school.

Joshua cleared his throat. "Ira and I were just going to have a bite of lunch. Would you gentlemen care to join us?"

Brian glanced at Dennis, who nodded. "We'd be honored." He wondered how Dobbs was faring with O'Hanlon. More immediately, he hoped that Ira had smoothed his way and that Joshua would not regard his visit as an intrusion.

6

PHILANDER DOBBS HAD followed Brian to Fall River in his own car.

"It may come in handy to have an extra vehicle," he explained. The truth was that though he had offered to be Brian's Watson, in his heart of hearts he fancied himself as Brian's Sherlock. And it was unthinkable for Sherlock not to have his own wheels.

He turned into the long driveway leading up the hill to Bowhead College. No imagination: It looked like a New England College ordered from a catalog. Redbrick—check. White trim and pillars—check. White-clapboard Colonial mansion on top of the hill. That had probably been the only building when it was a select seminary for young ladies of good family. He'd investigate it later when he went to pay his respects to Leander Seward, but first he'd mosey down to the greenhouses and see whether Finbar was around. He could usually be found in jeans and an old sweater, fussing around with his flats of seedlings or out in the beds demonstrating the correct way to trench or bed-out plants. He'd try the greenhouses first.

The parking area had one empty space. It was marked PRESIDENT SEWARD and had the Yale coat of arms stenciled under his name. Dobbs made a face and pulled in. Lee would have a fit if he saw him parked there.

The path to the greenhouses led down the hill, winding past a grove of maples decked out in fall colors. It skirted a good-sized pond, complete with ducks, and led on to a stone wall interrupted by a green wooden gate.

A red-lettered sign adorned with a skull and crossbones loomed above the neat fenced-in beds. DANGER! ALL PLANTS IN THESE BEDS ARE POISONOUS. STUDENTS MUST WEAR MASKS AND GLOVES AT ALL TIMES. STUDENTS ARE NOT ALLOWED TO WORK HERE WITHOUT SUPERVISION. WASH HANDS BEFORE RUBBING EYES OR TOUCHING FACE. THIS MEANS YOU!

A tiny man was on his knees, digging in a bed of *Colchicum autumnale.* He wore no gloves. His completely bald head was tanned to the same hue as his weathered face. His baldness was compensated for by bushy eyebrows and a luxuriant beard falling almost to his belt. Close-set, sharp brown eyes peered out from under this bushy overhang over an aquiline nose. His upper lip was short and turned up at the corners. Dobbs had never seen him out of jeans and a shrunken fisherman's sweater.

"Finbar, you old toxicist, what new horrors are you getting up to? Are you planning to slip some meadow saffron into Lee Seward's soup?"

"Don't tempt me. Good to see you, Dobbs." He wiped his hands on his knees and cocked an inquiring eyebrow. "What brings you here?"

"Do I need an excuse?"

"No, just a reason. You've been coming here for twenty years—every summer to see what I'm developing and every spring to pick out new varieties. This is the first time I've ever clapped eyes on you in October. Join me for lunch?"

"Pleasure."

"I usually brown-bag it, but I don't have enough to share. We'll go to the faculty club and give Lee heart failure when he sees the way I'm dressed."

Dobbs laughed. "You'll be disappointed. He must be off somewhere. I parked in his space."

"Then he'll have double heart failure if he comes back early."

The two men set off up the path, retracing Dobbs's earlier route.

"How are things at Bowhead?"

"Bad. Are you in a hurry for lunch? We could sit here by the duck pond for a few minutes while I tell you about it. There are some things it's not wise to discuss at the faculty club."

They sat on a green iron bench watching the duck squadron converge, eyeing them for handouts. Finbar produced a paper bagful of crusts. "Here you are, guys."

"About Bowhead?"

"Enrollment dropping, second-rate students, third-rate faculty."

"Present company excepted."

"Kind of you to say so. I've spent half my professional life building up Botany and Horticulture, but I'm afraid we're going down the tubes. It seems like fate, your showing up today. I was thinking of calling you. Want to invest in a college, or part of a college?"

"You take my breath away. I'd like to hear about it."

"And you shall, boyo, as my grandfather would have said in the ould sod. But you didn't come here for this. Don't tell me why just yet." The crusts were gone and the ducks looked reproachful. Finbar stood. "We'll talk in detail later. I just wanted to warn you to be discreet if we bump into Lee. I know you two were at Yale together."

"We were. The man was an ass then and it seems he still is."

It's worse than that; it's my opinion that he's gone off the deep end. Wait till you see the newly done faculty club."

Fittingly, the club was housed in a wing of the Colonial mansion on top of the hill. Double mahogany doors led off the great hall into a large dining room. Two huge Waterford chandeliers sparkled overhead, throwing subdued gleams off linenfold walnut paneling. Logs burned merrily in a fireplace surmounted by an Adam mantel. The glory of the fall sunshine was held at bay by dark red velvet drapes pulled across the tall windows. Dobbs assumed this was to underline the Waterford presence.

It was the portrait above the fireplace that made his jaw literally drop and his eyes pop. "Wha . . ."

Leander Seward loomed literally larger than life, heroic, posed in a scarlet gown of uncertain provenance. (To the untutored eye, it might be Oxford. Cambridge? St. Andrews? Or perhaps a bishop with a very imaginative tailor?) Crouched at his feet was a brace of anatomically improbable saluki hounds. A book was clasped to his bosom and his free hand rested gently on a grinning skull. Emblazoned behind him was the Yale coat of arms. The whole magnificent concoction was closed by a heavy Baroque frame.

One table stood in solitary splendor on a dais. It was unoccupied but set for two with heavy linen, fresh flowers, and what looked like genuine Spode emblazoned with the Yale arms, along with Yale-crested sterling. The tables for the lesser mortals were set with place mats and stainless steel.

"I see what you mean," Dobbs muttered, "a little touch of Leander in the night."

Finbar snorted. "The man's a megalomaniac."

"Even when we were lads, he had a swollen ego. I always thought he must be compensating for something."

Heads were turning. Several fastidious-looking fellows who sported campus-liberal tweed jackets with leather elbow patches over L. L. Bean or Lands' End turtlenecks raised supercilious eyebrows. Female professors exchanged glances. One lady of uncertain age swathed in a caftan offset by Birkenstock sandals—the campus bohemian—waved a hand and called, "Over here, Finbar. Join me."

"Thanks, but no thanks, Millie. Professor Dobbs and I have business to discuss."

A murmur rose behind them as he led the way to a corner table apart from the rest. "Dobbs? . . . Dobbs? . . . Not Philander Dobbs of Yale? . . . Lee will be sick to have missed him. . . . I hear they were classmates in New Haven. . . . What sort of business? . . ."

Finbar grinned evilly, "That's put the cat among the pigeons." The waitress handed them menus. "I can recommend the fish. Comes to us straight off the boat in New Bedford. The vegetables and salad are superb. Grew them myself, or my students did."

"Fish it is, then. Broiled scrod, baked potato, and salad, please." Finbar ordered the same.

"Now, why have you sought out an old gardener?"

"Am I right that you once told me you live in Fall River?"

"Sure do. The same house down on Globe Street that my grandfather bought. I bought the houses on either side and the one behind and tore them down, so I have room for a really good garden."

"Excellent. You may be just the man to help us. . . ." Dobbs filled him in.

"I may be able to help more than you realize. I sit on the board of the Delaney Institute."

Just as Finbar dropped this bombshell, the door opened and Leander Seward stood there practically gibbering with rage. "Who took my parking space? I just returned from an important meeting and . . ." His face was red and the wattles under his chin were quivering like a tom turkey's in rut. He had a full head of silver-white hair, popping blue eyes, and tended to embonpoint. If Dobbs had not known that he was a WASP to his toenails, he would have taken him for an old-fashioned Irish politician. He rose unhurriedly to advance with outstretched hand.

"Lee, my dear fellow, I'm afraid I'm the culprit. It was the only vacant spot. I didn't think you'd mind, since you obviously weren't using it. I'll go right out and move my car." His voice got plummier and plummier as he moved across the room.

President Seward seemed to dwindle and fold in on himself. "Phil Dobbs, is that you? I didn't mean . . . You're more than welcome. . . . I mean . . ." He gestured to the table on the dais. "I'll have the girl move your lunch to my table so we can have a chat." He snapped his fingers at the waitress, who was having a hard time keeping a straight face, "I'll have whatever my guests are having."

"Why, that's very kind of you, Lee. Professor O'Hanlon and I will be honored."

When they were ensconced with the linen, crested silver, Spode, and Waterford, their bottoms resting on black captain's chairs with the Yale coat of arms emblazoned on the backs, Dobbs gestured toward the portrait.

"Very handsome, but why the skull? I know you had the dubious honor of being a Skull and Bones man, along with our unlamented former President George Bush, but I would think you are old enough now to have put away childish things."

The remark was made lightly, so Dobbs was amazed at Seward's reaction.

"Childish!" he spluttered, little brown drops of coffee spraying across the table with his vehemence. "I know you've always jeered at Skull and Bones, but I'll have you know that I consider my membership the crowning achievement of my life at Yale."

Poor fellow, Dobbs thought, he really is far gone. "You can't mean it. Lolling in coffins to perform esoteric rites. You've got to be kidding."

Finbar's eyes swung back and forth between the two like a spectator at a tennis match and a hush fell over the other lunchers. All ears strained toward the dais.

"You'll find out."

"What will I find out?"

"Contacts, fellowship, brotherhood—that's what you don't understand. You never did." His face got a dreamy look. "No one understands. I have to save Bowhead, build it up. And I have a model."

"Seward, you're not making sense."

"I tried to start a chapter of Skull and Bones here at Bowhead. Do you know what happened? They wouldn't give me a charter; they laughed at me." His face had lost its high color and his chest wheezed.

Dobbs was alarmed; the man belonged in an institution.

42

Worse, he looked as though he was having a heart attack. He started to get up for help, but Finbar pulled him down.

"He's okay. Gets like this all the time, but it's psychosomatic. Doc Lawrence says he's sound as a bell."

Finbar had the right of it. Seward gulped down some water and his breathing returned to normal. "Sorry. It just is that I feel deeply about Skull and Bones. After all, Dobbs, how could *you* understand? I remember the day you turned down their bid, laughed at them. It was then they tapped me, so I owe you."

"Glad to be of service. But how is all this rigmarole going to help you save Bowhead?"

"Look what's happening in this country—the homeless, homosexuals, blacks, women: For God's sake, even the lesbians don't have the decency to stay hidden. They all want a slice of the pie." He winked knowingly. "Ask Finbar; he knows. Finbar has all the right instincts, even though he's Irish and comes to the faculty club dressed like a farmhand."

The answer still didn't make sense, but insulting more than half the population of the country seemed to settle him down. He turned a bland face to Dobbs. "I would like to take you on a tour of the college, dear fellow—and you must dine at my home tomorrow evening." The food arrived. It was as good as Finbar had promised.

7

"I'LL DROP YOU back at St. Fiacre's on my way to the Holiday Inn." Brian settled back and reached for his seat belt. "Buckle up."

Dennis tugged, but the standard belt would not accommodate his girth.

"What's your next step?" Dennis held the belt in place across his lap, hoping Brian wouldn't notice.

"Back to the motel in case Dobbs is there. There's no point my calling Detective Suarez, I have nothing to tell him, and cops don't welcome amateurs."

"I have a cop in my parish—Capt. Bill McGuire. He's head of the Holy Name Society and the parish council, an old-timer like you and me. More to the point, he's chairman of the board at Delaney. Want to meet him?"

"Nothing I'd like better. Just make it a social meeting; I wouldn't want him to know why I'm here. Were it not for the fact that I'm driving, I'd kiss you. As it is, you'll have to take the will for the deed."

He squirmed uneasily. "Don't talk about kissing me in front of Bill. He might take it the wrong way."

Brian whooped. "Why Dennis, are you hiding your preference?"

"I'll set up a meeting and let you know when. I can't ask you to dinner tonight. I have a meeting of the parish council. Bill McGuire will be there."

"And I have to touch base with Dobbs." He pulled up in front of St. Fiacre's. "Tell me, do you know anything about Bowhead College?"

"Only that they're in trouble financially."

"How about Finbar O'Hanlon?"

A guarded look passed over Dennis's face. "He lives in the parish. Why do you ask?"

"Just curious. He's been suggested as someone who knows the area."

Dennis hesitated a moment. "I really don't know him that well. I'll call you." He cut off further conversation by getting out of the car and heading up to the house.

As the Bard so aptly said, "The rest is silence," Brian thought as he pulled away. Maybe I got too close to the secrets of the confessional. Or maybe . . . The thought that reared its head appalled him. He gave himself a mental slap on the wrist and concentrated on his driving.

Dobbs was waiting at the motel, full of the news about the mess at Bowhead and Finbar's seat on the board of the Delaney Institute. Brian plunked himself down on the bed and stretched to full length.

"What do you think you're doing?"

"I'm going to take a little nap."

"At a time like this?"

"Nothing we can do right at this moment, but I applaud your eagerness." He rose on one elbow. "To misquote: I see you like a greyhound in the slip, straining upon the start. Now, let me catch a few z's."

Dobbs stood for a moment, irresolute. They should be doing something, but Brian's eyes remained firmly closed. With a shake of his head, he let himself out.

Brian was having a pleasant dream. His azaleas were being awarded first prize at the New York Botanical Garden. All the assembled gardeners were saluting him with their hoes and rakes as a brass band played "Hail to the Chief." Philander

Dobbs was green with envy. Maire was high-kicking in a Dallas Cowboys outfit. Then the brass band went flat and became an insistent bell. The telephone. He groaned and reached over to the bedside table.

"Donodio speaking."

"Brian, it's Ira. Joshua and I are still at the bookstore. Could you come back?"

"What's up?"

"The cops want to search the place and the media followed them over. We're besieged. God knows, we've had enough experience with reporters in the last few days, but Josh is in no shape to handle them, and I always lose my temper and make things worse for Liza."

"Did you call Liza's lawyer?"

"No. That should have been the first thing I thought of. See why we need you?"

"Call her the minute I get off the line. Do the cops have a warrant?"

"They say they do."

"Ask to see it, then try to delay them until the lawyer gets there. Dobbs and I will come as soon as possible."

"Gotcha."

Brian doused his face with cold water before he called Philander Dobbs. "Stir yourself, Watson. The game's afoot."

When they arrived at the bookstore, a gaggle of reporters surrounded Ira and no less than five TV cameras were focused on him. There was no sign of Joshua; he was probably inside. The idle, the curious, and the ghoulish crowded ten deep outside the low fence. A lone policeman tried in vain to keep order while his partner called urgently for backup over his car radio.

Some of the more enterprising souls perched in the trees with cameras clicking. Brian pushed through the throng to stand at Ira's side. He raised his hand.

"Ladies and gentlemen, Dr. Grossman has no comment to

46

make at this time. We are awaiting the arrival of Dr. Liza Borden's attorney."

A microphone was shoved into his face. "May we have your name, sir?" The speaker was a brash youth with remnants of adolescent acne. His hair was carefully layered on top, shaven at the sides, with a small ponytail sticking out to the rear. He wore a pale blue shirt opened to the third button to display a less-than-impressive chest festooned with gold chains. Without waiting for Brian's reply, he turned to gaze soulfully into the camera.

"This is Carleton LaPard coming to you from Borden's Books on French Street in Fall River. It is here that the husband of the alleged killer of Abby Meyer, Joshua Borden, runs what has been described as 'the best bookstore in Fall River.' In a bizarre twist on local history, the store is only a short distance from Maplecroft, the luxurious Victorian house on French Street purchased by Lizzie and Emma Borden when they inherited their father's fortune. With me now is Dr. Ira Grossman, the brother of the accused Liza Borden, and an unidentified friend." He shoved the microphone under Brian's nose again. "May we have your name, sir?"

"Certainly. I'm Dr. Brian Donodio. I represent the Borden family. As I said before, we are awaiting the arrival of Dr. Borden's attorney. Dr. Grossman is upset and does not wish to comment at this time except to say that he has full confidence in his sister's innocence."

This wasn't what LaPard wanted. He shoved the microphone into Ira's face. "Dr. Grossman, can you tell us why the police are searching the bookstore and what it is they hope to find? How will you feel if, while we are standing here, they find conclusive evidence of Dr. Liza Borden's guilt?"

Enough was enough. Brian snapped, "The same as your mother felt when she found out that her son had an IQ of fifty." A big grin spread over the cameraman's face. He kept the film running to assure that LaPard's discomfiture went over the airwaves in living color.

Standing to one side, Philander Dobbs observed. He deplored all this hype. He decided to take action. Police reinforcements had just arrived, but the officers were doing nothing to control the circus.

"Er, excuse me, Officer, may I have a word?"

"You can have as many as you want. What can I do for you?" The man had maneuvered into camera range and stood with legs apart, chin out, and gut in—the very model of Fall River's finest. He hoped his wife and all the relatives were watching.

"My name is Dobbs. I'm with Dr. Donodio and Dr. Grossman."

"Is that so?" A look of deep suspicion creased the officer's brow.

"And I was wondering . . ."

"No law against that."

"Against what?"

"Wondering."

"Er, yes." Dobbs felt as though he had wandered through the looking glass. "Can't you do something to make this bunch of yahoos behave?" His gesture encompassed the pushing media and unruly crowd.

"No way."

"What do you mean?"

"Freedom of the press, see? Like the people have a right to know. It's the American way." He slid around so his wife would catch his shiny holster on the tube. "It's as much as my job is worth to mess up freedom of the press."

The frustrating colloquy was broken up by a new arrival: a generously built woman of uncertain age swathed in an ankle-length red cloak. Upswept black hair formed a perch for a black felt sombrero. Knee-high boots, black tights, and a black leather miniskirt peeping through the opening in the cloak completed her ensemble. All heads swiveled. *Eye-catching* was an understatement.

Oh my, Dobbs thought, mutton dressed as lamb. He no longer needed to beg the cops to control the circus. The media knew when the ringmistress had arrived. Like a flock of migrant birds following the magnetic fields of the earth, they fell upon her with cries of delight.

When she was sure she had everyone's attention, she raised both arms above her head in a dramatic gesture for silence.

"You all know me. I am Rebecca Betancourt Delgado, Esq. I am Dr. Liza Borden's lawyer."

This was a woman who gave the viewing public value for their money! The first to reach her was a lissome female from ABC.

"Ms. Delgado, can you tell us—"

"Betancourt Delgado, darling. And you are . . .

"Kandy Kane, ABC News. Ms. Betancourt Delgado, can you tell us just what is going on here at Borden's Books? Why are the police here? Are they going to make any new arrests in connection with the ax slaying of Abby Meyer?"

"Darling, your guess is as good as mine until you let me go so I can find out what this new development is in the persecution of the family of my innocent client."

The media were in good hands. No one even noticed as Ira, Brian, and Dobbs slipped into the store.

8

REBECCA WAS MORE than capable of handling the lads and lassies of the networks. Brian knew he would only mess up her act if he hung around outside. It was more important to find out what was going on inside, where Joshua was trying to restore order to the main floor after the police search.

All the books had been pulled from the shelves and now lay in disordered heaps. From the floor above came the clumping of boots and disquieting bumps that told of similar mayhem being wreaked on the storeroom and office. As Brian stepped across the threshold, he tripped over a small volume bound in faded green cloth. He picked it up, smoothed it with automatic tenderness, and glanced at the title.

"My God," he exclaimed. The faded quarto was the 1855 first edition of *Leaves of Grass*. Whitman's name had not appeared on the title page, but W. Whitman was inscribed under the title in the great man's own hand. He placed the volume reverently on a shelf of the glass-fronted case reserved for rare books. When this was all over, he would inquire about its provenance and its price; now was not the time.

"Gentlemen, let's gather round the table. We have work to do." He pulled up a chair to the long oak display table in the center of the room and positioned a yellow legal pad retrieved from the mess on the floor. When all were seated, he held up his hand.

"Let's make a list." Brian was a great believer in lists. "First, what do we know?"

"We know that Abby Meyer was killed and that Liza didn't do it," Joshua almost shouted. "Why are we wasting time? We should be out doing something."

"We are doing something," Brian said soothingly. "Ira asked me to come here to help—I assume with your consent. So far, I know only what I've read in *The New York Times* and what Ira and you have told me on the phone and at lunch. Indulge me. Why was Ms. Meyer murdered? Did she pose a threat to someone? If so, to whom? Or was her death incidental to the main object of framing Liza?

"Is the killing tied to the Delaney Institute? Does it tie in with the disappearing bears and the mutilated animals? Did Liza or Abby, singly or in concert, find out something dangerous to the perpetrator?

"Is Bowhead College in the picture? I ask that because Finbar O'Hanlon is on their faculty and also on the board at Delaney and he's an authority on vegetable poisons. Above all, who benefits from this mess? Cui bono, as the legal eagles say."

"Won't the police investigate all this?" Dobbs rocked precariously back in his chair.

"Yes and no," Brian answered. "They'll probably continue to treat the Delaney mess as a separate case. Don't forget, they have their suspect in custody for the murder. They'll be looking for additional proof with which to crucify Liza, if you'll excuse the expression. Access to the weapon, a falling-out with Abby, that sort of thing. I wouldn't be the least bit surprised to find that the ax came from the Delaney toolshed."

Ira broke in. "What about motive? She didn't have one."

"What about it? Check with Ms. Betancourt Delgado, but I can tell you now that all the cops need is means and opportunity; motive is just icing on the cake. After all, Liza was literally red-handed when she was arrested. I think we need an eye and an ear right in the heart of the Delaney Institute. Ira, are you game?"

"Sure. If it will help Liza, I'm game for anything."

"Are you licensed to practice in Massachusetts?"

"I trained at Tuskegee, but I worked for a while when I first graduated at the Franklin Park Zoo in Dorchester. Yeah, I'm licensed."

"Here's what I want you to do. Get on the phone to Delaney right now before they have time to make other arrangements and volunteer your services as interim vet. Stress that you're doing it for your sister and you don't want any payment. Unless I'm very much mistaken, the 'no pay' bit will make them accept your offer with whoops of joy."

Dobbs watched with ill-concealed envy as Ira left the room. "What do I do?"

"You're our outside man. I think you should work on cultivating Leander Seward and Finbar O'Hanlon. There's probably no connection between Bowhead and Delaney, but they're linked by O'Hanlon. Go to dinner at Seward's tomorrow night. See what you can find out. Right now, we're working in the dark like the blind men and the elephant. Above all, soft-pedal my involvement."

Joshua looked more and more wretched as he listened to the plans. He raised his clenched fist and brought it down with enough force to make the table jump. "She is my wife and the mother of our children." His voice cracked. "What role do *I* have in all this?"

"You have the most important part of all. You have to keep Liza's spirits up."

"How? I'm not allowed to visit her while she's under indictment."

Brian was appalled. "That's inhuman."

"According to Rebecca, that's the law."

Joshua was a hell of a nice guy, but he struck Brian as just a tad ineffectual and too emotionally involved to be trusted with anything crucial to the investigation. He racked his brains for other jobs for him.

"You have to fend off the media. Then you have to coordinate everything the three of us do, keep Rebecca up to date on our shenanigans, and see that she keeps us abreast on what the police are doing. As Liza's husband, you have too high a profile to do any of the sneaking around. I'd like you to start by finding out if it's possible for me to visit Liza."

Ira stuck his head around the door. "You were right. They were a bit dubious about accepting my services, but when I said I was volunteering to do it for free, the ice thawed. The man I spoke to is Bill McGuire, the chairman of the board."

"That's Capt. Bill McGuire. He's also the head of the Major Crime Unit. Did he happen to mention if he was at Delaney in his capacity as chairman or as a cop investigating Liza?"

Two interruptions occurred simultaneously; the tramp of officialdom descending the stairs and the opening of the street door.

"Darlings," Rebecca announced, "here I am, ready to put my head together with your much wiser ones. First, let me have a word with the ladies and gentlemen of the law." She surveyed the mess. "I see they've done maximum damage in the search for God knows what." She disappeared into the tiny vestibule and they could hear scraps of her confrontation. A few words filtered through the thick oak: *harassment . . . warrant . . . complaint. . . .*

When she reappeared, there was a satisfied smile on her face. "They're sending someone over to clean up the mess, and I'm satisfied they found nothing."

"There was nothing to find," Joshua growled.

"Of course there wasn't," she agreed. "Now, introduce me to these lovely men and tell me what they can do for dear Liza."

After introductions, Brian outlined the plans he had thus far, ending, "I would like to visit Liza at Dartmouth. Can you arrange it?"

"I'll have to make you legal." She ran her hands through her upswept hair, dislodging her sombrero and scattering hairpins in a shower over the floor. "You're not licensed investigators, but I'll draw up agreements for you to sign that make you my employees as consultants. It's a bit dubious, but argu-

53

able, if it comes to that." She delved into her enormous shoulder bag and came up with three one-dollar bills.

"Here." She handed two bucks to Brian and one to Dobbs. "As soon as you sign the agreement, you are working for the accused's lawyer." She fixed them with a stern eye. "This means you're covered just as I am by the laws protecting privileged information. I'll try to get you in to see Liza tomorrow. I'll leave a message at your motel."

Despite Ms. Betancourt Delgado's outré appearance and splendidly colorful language, she reminded Brian of his third-grade teacher, Sister Mary John Paul. She had the same power to make him feel guilty of nameless transgressions. He thought she was a smashing lawyer and they were lucky to have her, but she was a tad overpowering. Besides, he was hungry.

"Gentlemen, madam, I must leave. It's been a long day and I fear it may be even longer tomorrow. Care to come with me to find some dinner, Dobbs?"

"As Rabelais so aptly quoted, *'natura vacuum abhorret.'* In other words, it's time to nosh. Would anyone care to join us?"

There were no takers.

"Any idea where we may find a decent meal?"

"Dennis told me about a Ukrainian place over on Globe Street that I thought we might try. He says the food is reasonable and decent. First, I'd like to find a phone and ask if he's able to join us for a while." Brian turned on the ignition and headed down to North Main.

"Why are we going this way?"

"Because it's the only way I know to a public phone. North Main becomes South Main. I know how to get from South Main to the bus station and I spied a phone booth outside the bus station. Ergo . . ."

As he waited for Dennis to come to the phone, Brian gazed across Second Street, where the original Borden house brooded in gothic gloom. He thought, Perhaps there is no

54

reason to this case, no cui bono. We may be dealing with a psychopath who could not resist staging an ax murder in Fall River when he realized he could frame another Lizzie Borden. Names are dangerous. What would happen to a man living in Whitechapel whose name just happened to be Jack Ripper?

"This is Father Duque."

"Dennis? Brian Donodio speaking. Philander Dobbs and I wonder if you would care to join us at that Ukrainian restaurant you told me about. . . . Yes, we know you have a meeting. . . . Fine, in about twenty minutes."

At first sight, the Uke as the locals called it, did not look promising. The building was constructed of dingy yellowish brick, its cavernous main entrance firmly closed with an expanding iron gate.

"Are you sure this is the place?"

"It's the address Dennis gave me. Maybe there's another entrance."

And so there was. Around the side and down a flight of stairs, a heavy door gave access to a low-ceilinged brick-walled barroom. It was lighted by red and green navigational lights cunningly wired to ships' wheels suspended from the beamed ceiling. A figurehead from the days of sail loomed over the bar, her impressive bosoms dominating the ambience. Mounted fish gazed reproachfully at the eaters. Those not lining the bar were seated at small wooden tables or in private alcoves.

Brian drew a deep breath. The smell was a heady mixture of beer, fish, grease, onions, and cabbage, with just a few trace elements thrown in.

"What do you think?"

Dobbs raised an eyebrow. "Cholesterol heaven. Promise you won't tell Emily?"

"Promise you won't tell Maire?"

"Deal," they agreed simultaneously.

"How many?" The waitress's Slavic heritage was plain upon her face: a heavyset young woman with high cheekbones and sky blue eyes under light brows and a frizzy nest of hair teased in the style of the early sixties. Evidently, the Uke did not go in for uniforms. Her generous bosom strained a black T-shirt that inquired plaintively, VOULEZ-VOUS COUCHER AVEC MOI ÇE SOIR? A possibly dangerous question in a city with a large French-Canadian population. Her equally generous behind tested the double-needle tailoring of Mr. Levi. The blue eyes sharpened.

"Say, didn't I see you two on TV this afternoon?"

Dobbs raised his eyebrows. "That was two other fellows. We're expecting someone to join us."

She led them to an alcove with room for four, then made a beeline for the bar. Brian watched her whisper excitedly to the bartender, then point to their table.

"Our fame has spread, damn it. Well, Dobbs, what's your next move? I have the inkling of a plan."

"Tell me . . ." His voice trailed off as he laid a restraining hand on Brian's arm. "Don't turn around. Finbar O'Hanlon just came in with another fellow. He told me he lives on Globe Street. There's a fat man just behind them. He doesn't have a Roman collar, but he's wearing those unmistakable black pants and he seems to know Finbar and the other guy. Would that be Dennis Duque?"

"Could be." Brian popped his head out of the alcove to peer. "Yes, that's Dennis." He half-stood and waved. "Over here, Dennis."

"Father Duque, Professor Dobbs."

"Professor." Dennis surveyed the booth. "In the interest of comfort, the two of you should sit on one side and I'll take the opposite. Or, why don't we ask for a larger table and see if Finbar and André would like to join us?"

It was inevitable, Brian realized. Dobbs had already spilled the beans to Finbar and would think it strange if the two parties did not merge.

The evening turned into a delight. All of the men but Dennis were keen gardeners, and Dennis had retained his boyhood attitude of interest in everything. By the time they were dawdling over coffee, he was discussing plans to revolutionize the landscaping at St. Fiacre's.

Finbar's friend answered to the name of André St. Cyr. A

fifth-generation Fall Riverite in his early thirties with the dark hair and liquid brown eyes of his French heritage, he lived with Finbar in the old house on Globe Street and managed the flourishing nursery garden Finbar had established.

Only one thing marred the party. From time to time, Brian caught dark looks from the bartender and a couple of rough-looking fellows, followed by muttered comments and hostile laughter. Finally he mentioned it.

"Don't all turn around at once, gentlemen, but I'm getting very bad vibes from that trio at the bar."

"It's because Finbar and I are known to be gay," André explained. "Why don't we go back to the house and hoist a few? It could turn ugly. No need to involve you guys."

The house was a venerable triple-decker set well back from the street in a huge yard surrounded by a white picket fence.

"Most of the places down here are crowded higgledy-piggledy on top of one another and this place used to be the same," Finbar remarked as he opened the gate to gesture them through. "I bought up the places on each side and in the back when real estate was cheap, then tore them down." He gave an expansive gesture. "André's family lived in one of the tenements and he worked for me. They bought a house in Tiverton, so he moved in here."

The door opened into a wide foyer with a staircase at the back. "Our office and salesroom are on the ground floor. We live upstairs. Welcome."

Upstairs was a revelation of what may be hidden behind the walls of an old-fashioned tenement. Finbar and André had gutted the central living room so it soared a full two stories to a vaulted ceiling. The bleached oak floor was polished to a high sheen and scattered with mellow Navajo rugs. Deep leather chairs and a sofa nestled cozily in front of the massive stone fireplace. André touched a match to the already-laid logs.

"Make yourselves comfortable. Do you have any preferences? I have some brandy I can recommend or some single malt."

When it was Dennis's turn to state his preference, he shook his head. "I find that the hard stuff doesn't agree with me anymore. I guess it's one of the penalties of age."

"How would you like to try our new drink? It's a top secret concoction of several different juices from genetically altered fruits, lightly carbonated. Finbar has been working on it in his lab."

"I'm game. If I turn blue and curl up my toes you can remember me as a martyr to science."

His drink was an unappetizing looking contrast to the various shades of amber in the other glasses. Dennis sniffed doubtfully at the murky gray liquid.

"It tastes better than it looks," Finbar assured him. "When I get the color problems caused by the mutated genes cleared up, André and I plan to patent it and go commercial. Close your eyes and swig."

Dennis obeyed orders. He took a deep swallow and a grin spread over his face. "It's perfectly delicious."

Brian glanced at his watch. "This is all very interesting, but I know that Dennis has a parish council meeting tonight and I have a few things I'd like to discuss before he has to leave. You all know why Dobbs and I are here?"

"I know what Dobbs told me," Finbar replied, "and so does André. He and I have no secrets."

Brian turned to Dennis. "I know you have to leave soon. You haven't told Bill McGuire about me, have you?"

"Not yet. Why?"

"Don't. I'd like to nose around a little without the police interfering. Sooner or later, they'd connect me with that business in New York and Ireland. It got a lot of publicity. Then they'd call New York and my daughter and son-in-law would hear about it and stick their two cents in. It's the sort of trouble I don't need. Stick your info under the seal of the confessional."

Dennis grinned. "Your theology is lousy, but I catch your drift." He drained his glass and lumbered to his feet. "I have to go. Good night, all. Mum's the word."

The four remaining talked far into the night.

BRIAN HAD NOT seen Liza Borden since her graduation from Prendergast, though Ira had kept him up to date on her progress. The image he carried was of a painfully self-conscious overweight teenager with acne and a ferocious overbite slowly yielding to a metal picket fence of orthodontia. He remembered how embarrassed Maire and he had been the first time she came to baby-sit. Deirdre had been terrified of the braces, associating them with a character called Jaws in a James Bond movie that she had seen on TV without Maire's knowledge.

The present reality was a slim redheaded woman in her mid-thirties. Even the atrocious prison garb could not conceal the disciplined litheness of her body. Her face was innocent of cosmetics and there were dark circles under her eyes. As she took her seat on the other side of the table, she clasped her hands together to still their tremor, but there was nothing she could do to still the tic under her left eye or disguise the savage biting that had stubbed her nails below the quick. Brian rose to his feet and bowed.

"Dr. Borden, or may I take an old teacher's liberty and call you Liza? I'm sorry we had to meet again in this place and under these circumstances."

She essayed a smile that didn't quite come off. "Liza, please. Dr. Donodio, it's so good to see you." She glanced at the correction officer, who moved out of earshot but stayed close enough to be an inhibiting presence. "Joshua and Ira sent word through Rebecca that you were riding to the rescue, but I really don't know what you can do."

"They're only allowing me fifteen minutes. Why don't you tell me in your own words exactly what happened."

"I've told it so often. The trouble is, no one believes me."

"I believe you. Certainly Joshua and Ira believe you, and a lot of other people. Actually, I think we'd be better served if I asked some questions that no one else seems to have asked."

"Fire away."

"Who would want to kill Abby Meyer? Whom did she threaten? Tell me something about her. I've heard her described as your best friend."

"Ira qualified at Tuskegee, but I went to Farmingdale, where I met Joshua." A smile curved her lips. "I wish you could have seen him then, nothing like the serious Orthodox Jewish gentleman he is today. The sixties were his spiritual home—long hair, beads, guitar, the whole bit. We were both raised as observant Jews, rebelled against it, and came back to it."

"We only have fifteen minutes."

"Well, to cut a long story short, we married at the end of our junior year and moved to Fall River after I graduated from veterinary school. Joshua's roots are here in Fall River and he always wanted to start a bookstore here. He was able to get the little red house cheaply. There'd been a fire and it was just a shell. He restored it completely. He made the research and restoration the subject of his doctoral dissertation in American history." She seemed lost in the memory of happier days.

He prodded her gently. "I'd love to hear the whole story someday. Very soon, I hope. Could we get to Abby?"

"Abby was the first friend I made at the synagogue in Fall River. She was just great. She was very into Greenpeace and Friends of the Earth—all that sort of thing. If there was a good cause around, Abby was for it. I'm a bit more hardheaded; I guess it's the scientific training."

"Where did Abby go to school?"

She made a deprecating face. "Bowhead. She didn't have what you could call a rigorous education, but she was happy. She did learn a lot about soil and plants from Finbar O'Hanlon."

There it was, Bowhead again. Everywhere he turned, Bowhead College seemed to be part of the story—Bowhead and Finbar O'Hanlon. "How did Abby get on the board at the Delaney Institute?"

"I proposed her name once I was settled in the job, and Finbar backed me up. Her family connections made her a shoo-in. I could count on those two being on my side in everything. I still can't believe she's dead."

"Are you sure it was Abby who called you that evening?"

"The person calling said she was Abby, but the voice was muffled and it sounded like a bad line. I didn't stop to think."

"Think now. Shut your eyes and put yourself back to the call. Could the caller possibly have been a man?"

She squeezed her eyes shut and supported her head with her hands. "I don't know. It could have been either. The voice was all muffled and it sounded sort of breathless and squeaky."

"Rebecca told us that the cops claim they responded to an anonymous call, and the tape backs them up."

"I know. And I have no witness to back up my story of getting a call at the bookstore." Her eyes filled with tears. "Dr. Donodio, they've got me coming and going. What am I going to do?"

"You're going to fight, that's what. And you've got a lot of people fighting for you. Now, for the sixty-four-dollar question: Do you think that the murder is connected with all the troubles at Delaney?"

It's the only thing I can think of, but how could killing Abby be connected with the troubles?"

"Maybe to frame you."

"That's ridiculous."

"What did Abby do for a living?"

"Sold real estate."

"Someone told me that Delaney was sitting on the largest parcel of desirable undeveloped land in the city."

"That's true. We've had lots of feelers from big developers, but Abby was never in that league."

"But she may have had contacts who were. Friends don't know everything. Tell me about her family connections."

"Her dad owns one of the biggest construction firms in the area. Their trucks are all over. 'Meyer the Builder: If it's Masonry, It's Meyer.' Her aunt Susan is our representative in the state assembly."

"Is she on the Highway Commission or the Appropriations Committee?

Liza's hand flew to her mouth. "How did you know?"

10

Brian sat on the bed while Dobbs got ready to dine at Leander Seward's.

"I wish you were coming."

"It's better if I don't. From what you tell me, Seward would be insufferably condescending to a mere Fordham Ph.D." He raised an amused eyebrow at Dobbs's splendor. "I still don't understand why you had to rent a tuxedo. Isn't it going a bit far?"

"I only wish I'd thought to bring my own rig. I hate the hang of this jacket."

"Nonsense. You look magnificent, a credit to Yale. Will anyone else be there?"

"I don't know. Certainly not Finbar; Seward has never invited him to the house. Finbar says it's because he's of Irish extraction and his father worked in the mills. Maybe it's because he's gay. Seward wouldn't dare fire him for that reason, but he may not want to socialize. I still don't know why you think Bowhead ties up with this mess."

"I don't either, except that every time I turn around, I trip over people connected with both institutions. Just keep your ear to the ground."

"And my hand on the plow?" Dobbs fastened the discreet ribbon of the Légion d'honneur in his buttonhole.

"That's the idea." Brian glanced at his watch. "Time you were leaving. Good hunting."

"Come home with my shield or on it?"

"You've got it."

Dobbs whistled happily as he drove east on U.S. 195, heading for Sandwich. Seward had given him precise directions. "You can't miss the house. Not far outside the town. Name on the gate is Seward's Folly."

Folly is the right word, he thought as he turned into the massive wrought-iron gates suspended between stone pillars. Either Bowhead is using all its income on the man's salary or he married money. He wasn't too well heeled at Yale, as I recall, and his family was nothing special. I wonder what Mrs. Seward is like? He leaned out to push the bell and announce himself over the intercom. The gates swung silently apart.

A long drive led forward through an avenue lined with huge rhododendrons that would be spectacular in the spring, ending in a graveled sweep in front of the house. No, he decided, not a house—a mansion. A château that would have been right at home in Bordeaux, built of gray stone, with a leaded roof and multiple chimneys. He was impressed; the sucker must have at least fifty rooms. As he reached the top step, the massive door was opened by a butler who looked as if he had been supplied by Central Casting in the 1930s.

"My dear fellow." Seward bustled forward, brushing aside the butler, who stepped back, face impassive. "Welcome. Come and meet Audrey. She's in the salon."

Dobbs followed, admiring Seward's full Highland evening dress. Was Seward a Scottish name? Probably some form of Stewart. He never paid much attention to such things. He thought it rather silly when one lived in America. Still, he was glad he'd come up with a dinner jacket, even if it was rented. He'd have hated to have had to apologize and give Seward a chance to be gracious.

Audrey Seward was not what he'd expected. A tall, forthright, and very ugly woman figged out in full Scottish regalia in the MacTavish tartan, she advanced through an obstacle

64

course of French Empire furniture thick with animal forms, bas reliefs, and caryatids.

"Professor Dobbs, I'm so glad to meet you. Leander has told me so much about you."

"The pleasure is mine."

"Do sit down. We just have time for a drink before dinner."

"In these surroundings I'd call it an aperitif."

She smiled. "It's a little overwhelming, isn't it? My late uncle's house. I always think it's a bit like lace ruffles on a leather jacket to have a place like this on the Cape, but Leander and I love it."

"It's just that . . ."

"I know. Totally out of keeping. I was orphaned very young. My uncle brought me up in this house and left it to me. We find a sip of aquavit before dinner perks the appetite. Will that be satisfactory?"

The table could have seated twenty in total comfort. The three of them huddled together at one end, served by the butler, who had managed a quick change into the full glory of tails and white gloves.

Dinner was a surprise. Judging by the ambience, Dobbs expected something Frenchified; frogs' legs or escargot, certainly haute cuisine. They started with squash soup, followed by a main course of roast chicken, cranberry relish, rice with just a hint of saffron, green beans, and a salad of wild mushrooms and young lettuce.

"You have a marvelous cook."

Audrey MacTavish Seward smiled happily. "I'm the cook. Leander keeps trying to hire someone, but I won't have it. I try to stick to the dishes of the region."

"A wise decision." He was desperately trying to think of a way to steer the conversation, hoping Seward, who was confining his contributions to grunts and smiles, would join in. He addressed him directly.

"Tell me, how much land do you have here? That avenue of rhododendrons must be a total joy when they're in bloom."

Seward was not interested in horticulture. He waved a

65

dismissive hand. "Audrey takes care of that side of things. We have a total of fifty acres—and we've divided it in half."

"Twenty-five acres each?"

"More or less. I keep my section wild, the way nature meant it to be."

Audrey snorted. "My husband is into male bonding. It's as much as my life is worth to cross over into his section of the grounds. His friends arrive for camp-out weekends, then come in from the wild on Sunday evening famished and full of bonhomie. I provide a smashing buffet before I retire with the *Times* crossword."

Dobbs's answering sally was stillborn. He glanced at Seward and there was a rapt look on his face, the look of a true believer.

"It's the only thing, Dobbs. Don't you ever long for the old days when a man could pit himself against nature, with nothing but his own skill and nerve between him and total disaster?"

"It must be very challenging."

"It's more than that; it's exalting. Then to gather round the fire with a few kindred spirits. Why, you know we went out one weekend when all we wore were loincloths. We took no food, hunted game with crossbows, and slept on beds of spruce tips."

"Came home covered with poison ivy and mosquito bites in places you didn't dare scratch," Audrey interjected.

Seward bridled like an angry horse. "You just don't understand. Why, once we sat and yarned until sunrise. And then do you know what we did?"

They had finished their main course, but the butler, who Dobbs had found out answered to the name of Mumford, was standing openmouthed at these revelations, too fascinated to clear and serve dessert.

"Tell me."

"We built up the fire, stood around it, and pierced our fingers with arrows. Then we mingled our blood and let it fall into the flames."

"And what did that accomplish?"

"It was a symbol, my good man. A sign that all men are blood brothers and share eternal maleness."

Dobbs shook his head. The man was crazy as a bedbug. "How does this philosophy of yours tie in with Bowhead College? And isn't this pitting yourself against nature eased a bit by doing it within walking distance of your house?"

A fleck of spittle appeared at the corner of Seward's mouth. Audrey laid a hand on his sleeve and murmured something too low for Dobbs to catch. He shrugged her off impatiently.

"You're like all the rest. You're scoffing. The greatest tragedy in America since FDR is the way that the white male has been denigrated in the last twenty years. Look about you. Women's studies, Afro-American studies, ethnic studies, multiculturalism." He slammed his fist down on the table, rattling the crystal. "Where, I ask you, are the Anglo-Saxon male studies? The Chinese and the Japanese know what I'm talking about. They want to keep their blood pure and they keep their women where they belong, but even they are being corrupted by our decadent ideas."

"Where do women belong?"

"Serving their men, that's where. It's nature's plan. And their men protect and provide for them. That's nature's plan, too. But you asked about Bowhead." His eyes grew cunning. "I want to make Bowhead into the first institution of higher learning entirely devoted to men's studies. That, too, is nature's way. Bowhead was started as a women's school, then it became coed. Now that the sexes have mingled there, it's time for the women to bring forth the men. See what I mean?"

Audrey had managed to catch Mumford's eye. Fresh fruit and a cheese tray suddenly appeared in front of them, sparing Dobbs from replying to this extraordinary and confusing statement.

"We'll have coffee in the living room later. Professor Dobbs, perhaps you would tell us something of your work at Yale? I understand you're an authority on endangered Caribbean species." She was trying valiantly to lighten the atmosphere.

67

Seward surfaced from a particularly juicy pear. "Never mind Dobbs's work. I want to get his opinion on my plans for Bowhead."

"Tell me more," Dobbs temporized.

"I already have a small program going and I bring some of the more promising senior students here for weekends. We hunt with longbows and crossbows and research some of the ancient male sports."

"Interesting."

"*Fascinating* is a better word. Fertility rites, tests of courage; we learn from other cultures that are still in touch with their male roots."

"Such as?"

"In spite of what you may think, I am not a bigot. For years, I have been a student of the Tao. I teach the young men the internal exercises and we practice them together—particularly the deer exercise, which embodies the tao of sex."

"I can see why your course might be popular," Dobbs remarked dryly.

"We also study Oriental healing practices. I myself can attest to some of their methods. I was quite rejuvenated by a treatment derived from ursine gall."

"Indeed?" Dobbs pricked up his ears. "Now *that* sounds fascinating."

"Yes. I had been incapacitated for years by a personal problem I won't detail. Suffice it to say that I switched to a Chinese physician, Dr. Chang, who practices in Fall River and got remarkable results after I was able to obtain the vital ingredient for his prescription."

Dobbs thought the whole rigmarole with the students sounded like a total disaster, but he could hardly say so. "How does your board feel about it?"

"My board is a bunch of backward-looking fools who are paralyzed by the bottom line. All they bleat about is money."

"Money does rear its ugly head in running an institution. Money aside, how do they react to your ideas?"

"They give them lip service. They know they have to tread softly with me."

68

"How so?"

"Money, of course." A dreamy expression spread over Seward's face. "Audrey graduated from Bowhead years ago when it was still a ladies' seminary. We have no children and she has left this place to the college, along with the finances to support it. The bequest is conditional on my continuing as president and living here. Isn't that so, my dear?" He reached out and covered her hand with his to give it an affectionate squeeze.

Audrey blushed like a maiden as she returned the squeeze. Dobbs was appalled. Audrey had better watch her back.

DEIRDRE DONODIO WAS worried. "Con," she called to her husband of one month and six days, "I don't like the way this dog is acting. I think we should take her to the vet." She eased herself off the cross-country ski machine that had been the one month-anniversary gift of her adoring husband and went into the bathroom, where he was shaving.

"Do you remember that old Anna Neagle movie where she played Queen Victoria? There was a scene where she and Prince Albert were newlyweds. She went into his dressing room and got all sentimental watching him shave. I always thought it was dumb, but now I see her point."

"And so you should, my queen. And seeing that you're my queen, isn't it about time you started calling yourself Connolly?" Con caught her around the waist and bestowed a lathery smooch on her lips. "Now you have a mustache."

"Yuck! You know we agreed that I was keeping my own name. I like it." She struck an attitude beside the tub.

"Does your hubby misbehave? Come home late and rant and rave? Shoot the brute with Burma Shave." Before he grasped her intent, she grabbed the can of shaving cream and caught him full in the face and down the chest.

"Gotcha!" she crowed, and ran from the room, with Con in hot pursuit.

"Now I have you my proud beauty." He dashed the cream off his face and leered.

"Unhand me."

"No way." He chuckled evilly as he steered her toward the bed.

Sometime later, she returned to the subject of the dog. "I really don't like the way Mdeb looks. She's not eating, her nose is hot, and her coat looks awful."

"I know and I'm worried too. The trouble is that her regular vet is on vacation and I can't stand his partner."

"Why don't I call Ira?"

"Who's Ira?"

"You met him at the wedding."

"I must have met three hundred new people at the wedding."

"Ira Grossman. He used to be one of Dad's students at the Prendergast School; now he's our vet and a friend of the family. His office is in Far Rockaway. I know it's a long drive, but I'd feel better about her if we had some advice. He could tell us if it's safe to wait or if we should bring her in."

"You're right."

Ira was not available. Deirdre got an earful from Dr. Duffy. She hung up thoughtfully. A few minutes later, she called Maire in Kansas City.

12

BRIAN HAD BEEN holed up for four days at Finbar and André's house and he was starting to look thoroughly scruffy. A four-day beard, thrift-shop clothes, and no showers are wonderfully convincing—particularly when a man works up a good sweat helping out in a nursery business. Now it was time to put his disguise to the test. Brian had wondered how he could get on the inside at the Delaney Institute to do a little snooping. When Finbar mentioned a staff opening for a groundsman and said he would recommend him, Brian leapt at the idea. Fortunately, Maire was delayed in her return from Kansas City. When he'd called her the previous evening, he had urged her to stay as long as she needed.

"Are you up to something dangerous already?" Her voice had a suspicious ring.

"No. Philander Dobbs and I are having a marvelous time with a couple of other gardeners. You might call it a male-bonding ritual."

"Male bonding, my foot. You wouldn't know a male bond if it bit you. You're up to no good, and I know it."

Today was the day. He had an appointment at ten o'clock with a Mr. Bevilaqua, the head gardener of the forty-five-acre preserve. Brian gave himself a final check in the mirror:

Haircut: needed
Shower: ditto
Glasses: his prescription shades
Sneakers: disgraceful
Jeans: dirty
Sweatshirt: Harvard
Beard: scruffy
Fingernails: ragged
Watch: plastic digital
Hands: filthy
Socks: K Mart
Baseball cap: Red Sox

He knew from Finbar that the Delaney Institute was spending so much on security that they couldn't afford to be too fussy about whomever they hired to do hard work at minimum wage. He also knew the interview was a formality. Finbar had already told the board that he'd known Brian for years and could vouch for him. He was an eccentric old coot and none too clean, but a good worker.

The eccentric old coot got off the bus pretending not to notice the obvious relief of the other passengers when he signaled for the stop, but he could feel the heat of shame rising around his ears. It was the first time in his life that people had moved away from him because of his body odor. Oh well, he thought, all in a good cause.

Wrought-iron gates hung between stone pillars proclaimed the entrance to the Delaney Institute. They were guarded by a teenager in khaki holding a walkie-talkie. He eyed Brian with disdain as he ambled up to the entrance.

"Keep moving, bud. This here's private property."

Brian stiffened to blast the oaf with a few well-chosen words, then remembered the part he was playing and reached to scratch under one arm. The boy moved hastily backward.

"Is this here the Delaney place?"

"What's the matter"—the boy gestured to the sign—"can't you read?"

"I have an appointment with"—he dug a creased, grubby paper out of his pocket—"Mr. Bevilaqua."

"Oh yeah? What's the name?"

"Brian MacMorrough." He had decided to use his first and middle names instead of a complete alias.

Muttered words were exchanged on the walkie-talkie. "Straight up the drive, first building on the right." The gates swung open.

"Much obliged." Brian scratched again, this time on his gluteus. "What's your name?"

"What's it to you?"

Really, it was nothing to him. He sighed and started up the driveway, the lifts inside his sneakers altering his usual loping stride into a mincing shuffle. Right inside the gate to the left was a two-story Tudor-style cottage that must be Liza and Joshua's house, where Ira was staying. He wondered whether he'd be able to grab a few words with him today in the course of his grounds-keeping chores. Would a humble hourly worker hobnob with a mighty vet?

The garden surrounding the gatehouse was brave with fall flowers and the climbing Cécile Brunner rose trained above the door was in the full beauty of its second flowering. He recalled that this variety had been developed in France in the late nineteenth century. This was an ancient polyantha, perhaps brought back from the grand tour by some sprig of Yankee nobility? What a pity Liza could not enjoy it.

It was not far from the gatehouse to the utility building—a neat but characterless wooden rectangle painted white with green trim. Within were tractors, power mowers and tools, large and small, manual and powered, lined up in rows. A desk was shoved into one corner. Behind the desk was a trim, dark middle-aged man.

"Mr. Bevilaqua?"

Bevilaqua, to his credit, did not flinch or race to fling the windows wide. He rose and came around the desk with outstretched hand.

"You must be Mr. MacMorrough. You come highly recommended by Mr. O'Hanlon. Have a seat and let's get down to business." He retreated behind the desk and started shuffling papers. "There are a few formalities we have to go through to keep Uncle Sam happy. Social Security, W-four form for the IRS, and proof of citizenship or your green card." He smiled expectantly and held out his hand.

Brian hadn't thought ahead. I should have done so, he thought ruefully, but maybe I can get away with supplying my Social Security number and promising to hand in the other stuff later.

"Hell, I'll have to write to my sister and ask her to mail me all that stuff. Traveling around the way I do, I like to know it's all safe with her. Tell you what—I know my number by heart. I'll give you that to start with and hand in my papers later." He paused hopefully.

Bevilaqua shook his head. "It will have to do, I guess. Mr. O'Hanlon tells me you're a good worker, and we are way behind. Come over here and take a look."

He rose from behind the desk and went to a large-scale map that covered one wall. "The Delaney Institute covers forty-five acres. The main house is here." He pointed to a rectangle. "The garden and lawn in front of the house and the outbuildings, including the area for the animals, take up about six acres. The rest is mainly fields, though we do have a stand of virgin timber."

Brian was keenly interested. "Cropland? Do you grow your own fodder?" He realized that he sounded more educated than he should. Bevilaqua shot him a quizzical glance.

"As much as possible. Of course we have to import for some of the exotics, but that won't be any concern of yours. Our crops are corn, hay, and assorted vegetables. There's a small apple orchard. You'll be concerned with routine care of the crops and the grounds. Now, if you'll come with me, I'll give you a uniform and assign your locker. You'll have time for a shower before you put on the uniform."

On the way to the locker room, Brian ventured to ask, "That pretty house down by the gate? Is that where Lizzie Borden lives?"

Bevilaqua stopped dead and poked Brian's chest with a

stiff finger. "Not Lizzie Borden; it's Dr. Liza Borden to you, and don't you forget it! She didn't do it and I don't care what those idiot police say. They should be finding out who's abusing our animals and trying to frame Dr. Borden as a murderer. And if I hear one more word out of you about the case, O'Hanlon or no O'Hanlon, you're fired."

Touchy, aren't we? He chewed over Bevilaqua's fiery defense of Liza as the welcome warmth of the shower sluiced down his back. The man was right in not wanting to discuss things with an ignorant old duffer, but maybe he'd open up to Ira as vet pro tem. He'd have to suggest it if he could grab a private word with Ira. Is Bevilaqua defensive because he's on Liza's side, or is it because he's implicated in what's going on? The man's in a perfect position to cooperate in all sorts of nastiness.

Feeling ten pounds lighter and much more comfortable, Brian toweled himself and donned the clean underwear he'd stuck in his pocket. On reflection, he left the beard. A man has a right to grow a beard, doesn't he? The green twill pants and the shirt embroidered on the back with DELANEY INSTITUTE fit only where they touched, but they were infinitely better than the noisome rags in which he arrived. He presented himself again at Bevilaqua's desk.

"All set?"

"I am."

"Good." He pointed with his chin at a man standing to one side. "This is Steve Springer. He'll show you the ropes. Steve, this is Brian MacMorrough. Get him started."

Springer was a taciturn type. He grunted to acknowledge the introduction and jerked his thumb at two large gasoline-powered leaf blowers. Fortunately, they were the same make as Brian's own machine in Woodside.

"Where do I dump the leaves?"

"Bins behind the shed. We'll shred them later for the compost."

"Lots of compost." Brian pointed to the expanse of lawn adrift with the fallen leaves of oaks, maples, and other deciduous trees and shrubs.

"We use lots of compost."

Brian was enjoying himself. The air was brisk but not cold, the sun pleasantly warm through the back of his shirt. He pushed the blower back and forth in ever-diminishing sweeps as he drew closer and closer to the front of the main building, pausing now and then to haul his sacks of leaves to the bins in back of the maintenance building. He was building a ferocious appetite. A glance at his watch told him why; it was after two o'clock.

After he delivered his last load of leaves he looked for Springer or Bevilaqua, but neither man was in evidence. He decided to explore.

Where to start? The main building was the obvious choice. A Greek Revival mansion in the high style with a portico supported by six Ionic columns, their volutes shouldering a wildly ornate entablature carved with nymphs and satyrs engaged in questionable activities. They would certainly upset the horses. More power to them. He laid a hand on the elaborately carved walnut door and pushed.

The paneled hall led to a magnificent broad staircase that rose for a good twenty feet, then branched off to both sides as though floating on air. But the way was not without its guardian dragon.

"May I help you?"

The speaker was in what is called the prime of life and broad of beam. Her shelflike bosom supported a pair of gold-rimmed glasses on a chain and her hennaed hair was teased into an overpowering mass over shrewd blue eyes and a bulbous nose. The eyes were fixed on his dirty sneakers.

He supposed he couldn't blame the woman. Even in his clean uniform, he looked less than prepossessing. "Excuse me, Miss, my name's MacMorrough. I just started here today. You wouldn't happen to know where a man can get a bit of lunch around here? I'm getting awful hungry."

She raised her eyes to the ceiling and tssked through her teeth. "I wasn't told we had a new employee. Didn't Mr. Bevilaqua tell you the rules?"

He whipped off his cap and held it humbly over his heart.

"No, Miss. I wasn't told nothing. What do I do about lunch?"

She tapped the desktop with her pencil just as Sister Imelda used to do when he was in fifth grade. "Outside staff is not allowed to use the front entrance," she said, glancing at the polished parquet and back at his offending sneakers, "for obvious reasons. We do have a staff lounge where you may eat your sandwich, but no food is served. Most of us bring our lunch from home."

"How was I supposed to know that?" He allowed himself to sound faintly truculent.

"You should have asked when you made the appointment for your interview. Planning, man, planning. What kind of help are we getting these days?" she asked rhetorically. "They don't think of the most obvious things."

"Who is this fellow, Mildred?"

Brian turned to survey the man who had come up soundlessly behind him. Tall and heavy, he nevertheless had the ability to move as silently as a cat. His head was crowned with a thicket of white hair and his eyes flickered restlessly, missing nothing. Cop's eyes, Brian thought, remembering his own father, Capt. Antonio Donodio of the New York City Police. His short Irish nose and dew-lapped cheeks showed the fine network of broken capillaries that usually presage the heavy drinker. He made a silent bet with himself that this was Captain McGuire, chairman of the board and the officer in charge of the investigation in Abby's murder. He won the bet.

Mildred's hand flew to her magnificent breastworks. She tittered like a teenager. "Captain McGuire, how you startled me coming up like that. This is Mr. MacMorrough. He just started here today as a groundsman. And I really must complain. Mr. Bevilaqua didn't tell him any of the rules. Why, he didn't even know that he's not supposed to use the front entrance."

"Okay, okay, you can't blame a man for doing what he didn't know he shouldn't. I'll speak to Bevilaqua."

"Oh, Captain McGuire, you're always so kind. But I do think that common sense . . ." But McGuire had turned his back on her.

Brian twisted his cap in his hands. "I'm sorry, mister. I didn't mean no harm. All I wanted to know was where I can get a bite to eat. I won't never come in here no more." Was he laying it on too thickly? No, McGuire seemed to accept him at face value. He edged a little closer and sniffed: bay rum, talcum, the slight aroma of good woolen cloth, and, sniff, sniff—by God, the man had taste. A touch of Glenties single-malt whiskey—his own favorite tipple. Maybe he'd been too quick to dislike the man.

"You're the fellow O'Hanlon recommended?"

"That's right, sir."

"Where are you from?"

The essence of a good lie is to tell as much of the truth as possible. "I guess you could call me a rolling stone. I was born in New York City, down in the Rockaways."

"Known O'Hanlon long?"

"Off and on for a few years. You might say we're in the same line, so to speak."

"How do you mean?" McGuire's gaze sharpened and one eye closed in a knowing wink.

He knew what the wink was about, but damned if he'd bite. "I've helped him out over the years. See, I'm like what you could call a jobbing gardener. Always like to have my hands in the dirt, but nothing like O'Hanlon. I ain't had the learning and never had the luck to get a place of my own. I was hoisting a few in a joint called the Uke a few nights ago and ran into him. He told me about the job and said he'd speak for me."

"I see. Come along with me, my man. I'll see if I can find you something to eat. I'm here today on police business, and one advantage of being a captain is being able to send a patrolman out for sandwiches. Can't have our new employee starving on us." Brian essayed a grateful smile and a respectful shuffle. "I noticed how clean the front lawn looks as I came in. Your work?"

"Yes, sir."

They left Mildred looking scandalized at the great man's condescension.

13

It's all very well for Con, Deirdre fussed. She had hours to kill before he came home from doing all the things detective sergeants do when they're assigned to homicide in the New York City Police Department. She thought, Maybe I was wrong to quit my job as an investigator with the INS.

I've got to find a job soon, she decided. This housewife stuff is for the birds. Meanwhile, she was sure her father was up to his ears in mischief in Fall River. Sherlock Donodio, supersleuth! Dr. Duffy had known nothing of Brian's possible involvement in the Liza Borden case, but he had been a mine of other information about Ira Grossman's activities in Fall River and had given her all the gossip while he treated Mdeb.

Mdeb! She glanced at her watch. Time for her medication. The old Irish setter was recovering nicely but still had to be helped up and down the stairs when it was time for her necessary walks. Deirdre sighed as she dipped the pills into one hand while she forced Mdeb's mouth open with the other and slid them onto the back of her tongue. A long run might lighten her mood. After walking the dog, she'd go for a run over by FDR Drive and time herself as far as the Triborough Bridge and back.

Mdeb was in no hurry to do her business. She creaked

along arthritically, stopping several times to consider and reject likely sites for her benison or to exchange rude sniffing courtesies with other dogs. The clock was striking two before Deirdre set out on her run.

Four honeymoon weeks of throwing coins in fountains, lounging in gondolas, and shopping in Florence do nothing for a girl's wind and legs, great though they are in other respects. She decided to cut her run short at Fifty-ninth Street and the Queensboro Bridge. She had only reached the Midtown Tunnel and already her lungs were a streak of fire, her legs felt like cement blocks, and a stitch gnawed at her right side. Sweat rolled off her in freshets. She slowed to a lope and concentrated on her situation.

It would be at least six months until the next police examination and it could be a couple of years before she worked her way up the list. No way she wanted to be a firefighter or a corrections officer. Teach? Teaching jobs were hard to find and she didn't think she had the inclination or the patience. Office work? Forget it! The first time she was expected to bring her boss coffee or dust his or her desk, she'd walk out. Social worker? Professional social activist? Closer, but not quite the ticket. One thing she did know: She wasn't going to spend the time waiting for an appointment to the cops by washing Con's socks and dusting the bookcases.

Maybe her mother would have some ideas, but she was in Kansas City having fun at the Blessington. Maybe she could be Maire's assistant? No, that would be a cop-out. The immediate problem was Dad up there in Fall River, doing God knows what.

She'd tried to get hold of Ira at the number Dr. Duffy supplied but reached only a machine. He had not returned her call. Probably Brian told him not to. Maybe Con should call and have a word with the force in Fall River? No, Dad would never forgive them. One thing was sure: He could never be convinced that an old Prendergastian could become an ax murderer. Well, the honeymoon was over. She'd tell Con tonight that she was leaving for Fall River first thing in the morning.

The shadow of the Queensboro Bridge fell over her. She realized that she was running easily.

14

CONFERENCE TIME. BRIAN eased his aching muscles against the back of his chair and surveyed his crew gathered around Finbar's kitchen table. Finbar was in his old jeans and a ratty T-shirt, his arm flung carelessly around André St. Cyr's shoulders. Philander Dobbs puffed ruminatively on his smelly old meerschaum. Dennis Duque was in full clerical attire. Ira Grossman and Joshua Borden had their heads together over the latest media enormity. And finally, there was Rebecca Betancourt Delgado, Esq., the only member on the distaff side. They were a motley conglomerate of talents indeed. He cleared his throat and rapped on the table for attention.

"Ms. Betancourt Delgado, gentlemen. I think the time has come for us to pool our knowledge in a systematic way. What is called, in modern parlance, a think session."

Dobbs grimaced. "How about a game plan?"

"It's no game, guys." Ms. Betancourt Delgado rose to her feet. She looked softer and younger than the last time Brian had seen her, at the bookstore. Her hair was pulled back in a long braid and her face was void of makeup. Instead of her eye-popping public garb, she wore a pair of old jeans and a man's work shirt. "My client is charged with murder and the cops have means and opportunity. The media is having a field day, as you well know. Liza says she was framed, and I believe her. But what can I do? Hers are the only prints on the weapon. We have no witnesses to testify that Abby told them she was going to call Liza, so it's only Liza's word against the evidence. I'll do what I can with lack of motive, but, as I've explained over and over, the prosecution does not have to prove motive when they have means and opportunity—and they have those in abundance." She gave her hair an indignant toss before she plopped back into her seat.

It was too much for Joshua. He pushed back from the table and bolted from the room, followed closely by Ira. Brian sighed. He had to find something to keep Joshua busy and out of their hair. The poor guy was in a lousy predicament, but in his present mental state he would be a real drag on the investigation. He made a note to confer later with Ira about Joshua. He coughed to draw their attention.

"I've been thinking. We have two institutions, Bowhead College and the Delaney Institute. At first glance, they seem to have nothing to do with each other, but they both keep cropping up.

"Finbar here is on the board at Delaney and on the faculty at Bowhead. Abby Meyer, God rest her, graduated from Bowhead and was on the board. We all know that Bowhead is in serious trouble—slipping reputation, lack of financial stability, and a kook for a president. It looks as if someone is out to destroy the Delaney Institute by ruining its reputation as a research facility and as a safe haven for endangered birds and mammals or, indeed, for any animal.

"We know that Delaney is sitting on forty-five acres of prime real estate and that Abby's father is the Meyer of Meyer the Builder, Inc., and that her aunt Susan is Representative Meyer at the State House in Boston. Now, has anyone any idea of how to tie all this together?"

Before anyone could speak, the door opened and Ira poked his head in. "I took the liberty of bedding Joshua down upstairs. He hasn't really slept since Liza was arrested. I gave him a sleeping pill."

Brian nodded. "Best thing in the world for him. Phil Dobbs

has a report to give, and I think you'll find it provocative. Go ahead, Dobbs."

"I had the mixed pleasure of dinner at Leander Seward's place. Totally weird, as the kids would say." He filled them in rapidly. "Here's what I got out of it. Mrs. Seward is a very nice woman who is utterly besotted with her husband. She's remarkably ugly and I'll bet he was the first man who ever gave her a tumble. She has the money and, from their setup, I'd say that it's a considerable pile. No children—they haven't been married long and she's a bit over the age.

"Anyway, Seward told me that the trustees at Bowhead can't kick him out because her will leaves all the money to Bowhead, with the proviso that he remain lifetime president."

"Mrs. Seward had better watch her back," Finbar remarked.

"My sentiments exactly. Also, they have fifty acres out on the Cape and they divide it in half. She never trespasses in his section."

Finbar chuckled. "What does old Seward do with twenty-five acres? He doesn't know a rake from a hoe."

"Runs male bonding soirees—drums around the fire, all that sort of stuff. And he greatly admires the traditional Oriental attitudes toward women. In fact, he's got some sort of Oriental connection. Swears by a Chinese doctor called Chang here in Fall River, says he treats him for some nameless condition with an extract made from ursine gall."

Ira snapped to attention. "You don't say?" he murmured.

Dobbs gave a predatory grin. "I thought it was interesting, to say the least."

Brian rubbed his hands together. "I have a sneaky plan. Rebecca, you're an officer of the court. I suggest you don't need to know what we're planning."

"I can take a hint." She gathered her papers. "Just keep me informed of the ends. The less I know about the means, the better."

15

"NOT AGAIN!" CON sat back and glared at Deirdre across the kitchen table.

"Well, I don't know for sure, but I have a strong suspicion." She pushed her long blond hair away from her eyes and grinned at her lord and would-be master. "So, I decided that I'll take a run up to Fall River and spy out the land. You can join me on your days off."

"We're only just back from our honeymoon," he protested. "Would you desert me before the ink is dry on our marriage certificate? Come here, woman."

"Keep your lecherous paws to yourself. You know I only married you because I wanted half of a Manhattan brownstone." She pulled away, but not very convincingly. "Well, maybe not just for the house," she conceded a few minutes later. "I must admit that I like it when you get all masterful."

He looked around at the airy kitchen with its 1930s green-and-cream enameled stove, green-sprigged curtains, and turn-of-the-century pine cabinets they had relieved of generations of paint. "I didn't marry you to get a housekeeper, but I love the house you keep. How long until dinner?"

"Soon. Why? What did you have in mind?"

"Do you have to keep watching it?"

"So that's what you have in mind."

Sometime later, she sat up in the big brass bed and sniffed. "I smell smoke. Oh Lord, the casserole."

"I don't smell a thing." He reached up a long arm. "Come here."

But she was zipping down the stairs.

"Julia Childs never cooks in the altogether," he observed as he came up behind her.

"Shush up, you. Open the window. No, don't. Someone might see us." She dumped the charred pan in the sink and raced out of the room, returning with two bathrobes. "Here, put this on. Now open the window."

"Who's to see us?"

"Your mother and sister might be out in the garden."

"And they'd see a fine sight on a chilly evening." He shrugged into his robe and threw open the sash.

"We'd better get dressed and go out to eat. And we still have to decide what to do about Dad."

"What's to decide? You have to go and I'll join you on my days off. Meanwhile, do you think I should have a brotherly word with the boys and girls behind the badge in Fall River?"

16

"WHAT SHALL I say is the matter?" Philander Dobbs checked himself in the mirror. "I think I look damn healthy."

Brian grinned. "Since Seward was so evasive about the ailment this Chinese wizard cured for him, I'd say it is a safe bet that he couldn't get it up anymore. Why don't you indicate a similar problem. That way, you can look perfectly healthy and still be taken seriously."

"Emily would be furious."

"What Emily doesn't know won't hurt her—and remember, you invited yourself in on this caper. I never said it would be easy." He checked his watch. "I have to go or I'll be late for work and Bevilaqua could fire me. What time is your appointment with this Dr. Chang?"

"Nine o'clock."

"Well, you'd better get a move on, and so should I. Have fun."

Dobbs drew up in front of Dr. Chang's office on June Street with five minutes to spare. The place looked innocuous, a restored carpenter Gothic house fronted by a wide porch. It was painted in ochre with canary yellow trim and surrounded by a neat but unimaginative garden. The sign over the bell read, WILBUR CHANG, M.D., P.C. WAIT FOR THE BUZZER. He rang and waited for the door to be released.

A middle-aged Chinese nurse smiled as he came through the door. "Mr. Dobbs?"

"That's right."

"Please take a seat, the doctor will be with you in a few minutes. While you're waiting, you may fill this out." She handed him a clipboard with a questionnaire.

The questions were routine, nothing to cause a raised eyebrow. The waiting room was immaculate. The nurse dealt competently with a busy phone. Maybe he was offering his precious bod on the altar of a mare's nest, to mix a metaphor. When he returned the clipboard, the nurse handed him a paper cup.

"Through that door. After you bring back the specimen, I'll weigh you."

Specimen obtained and weight ascertained, he was conducted to the sanctum sanctorum. Dr. Chang came from behind his desk with outstretched hand. The man was very tall and thin as a spider. A domed forehead loomed over almond eyes of emerald green. He moved like a cat. The white lab coat seemed utterly incongruous. He should have been wearing a silk jacket and a skullcap topped with the coral bead of a mandarin. Shades of Sax Rohmer, Dobbs thought, Fu Manchu incarnate. Unfortunately, I'm no Nayland Smith, but it might be wise to check for a stray dacoit.

"Mr. Dobbs, I'm Dr. Chang. It's nice to meet you. Please, sit down. Now"—he picked up the questionnaire and scanned the data—"all this seems to be very normal. What, specifically, is the problem?"

Dobbs squirmed in his seat. Brian was going to pay for this. "Well, er, I'm getting on, you know. Not as young as I used to be."

"None of us is, alas."

"I was given your name by Leander Seward. He told me you had done wonders for him with a similar problem. So, I thought . . ."

"No two problems are exactly the same, Mr. Dobbs, even if they seem to be, but let me hazard a guess at yours. Is it maybe connected with your ability to relate to the fair sex?"

"Er." He looked around for inspiration. There was something odd about this office after all. The walls were covered with pictures of bears: pandas, grizzlies, Kodiaks, black bears, polar bears—there was even a bearskin rug on the floor.

"I see you're admiring my bears."

"They're very beautiful animals."

"And a potent symbol of healing among my people. Unfortunately, they are getting harder and harder to find in the wild. But come, let us go to the examining room and we can talk some more while I see if I can pinpoint your trouble."

"Frankly, I'm scared to death." Ira Grossman checked his veterinary equipment with special attention to the tranquilizing gun. "I mean, wouldn't it be wiser to tell the cops what we suspect?"

"I agree with Ira. After all, Bill McGuire is the president of my parish council. How will I explain if we're caught?" Dennis was sweating so hard that his clerical collar was wilting.

Brian, too, had qualms, but he was not about to let them show. "Appealing to the cops is a one-way ticket to nowhere. We have no evidence and they'd laugh in our faces. Look at Dobbs, Finbar, and André; they think we have a good chance of bringing it off, but we'll have no chance at all without St. Fiacre's work van and Ira's expertise. Now, Dobbs is the one who's been there. He's prepared a map. . . ."

Earlier in the evening, the light of the harvest moon nearly led to the cancellation of the plan. Now the storm forecast earlier was whipping in from the east, bringing falling temperatures and comforting darkness. Brian consulted his watch.

" 'That which thou wouldst do, do quickly,' as St. John so wisely observed. Bless the National Weather Service." Humming "With Catlike Tread," he led the black-clad sextet to the van parked outside St. Fiacre's. Dennis Duque took the wheel and Dobbs navigated; the rest piled into the back with Brian.

"Let's go over the plan one more time. We all have walkie-talkies, thanks to Dobbs's American Express card. Ira, Dobbs, Finbar, André, and I will go looking for the enclosure or barn where, if our theory is correct, Seward is holding the stolen bears. Dennis will stay with the van. If we find them, he'll bring the van as close in as possible, load up the animals, and return them to the Delaney Institute. If we can't get close enough to spring them, we take pictures for the Animal Rescue League and let them notify the cops. If we don't find anything, we've goofed." As he finished speaking, the first drops of rain splashed down on the roof of the van.

For a long time, they rode in silence, each busy with his own thoughts. Brian knew how hard it was to go against the law-abiding habits of a lifetime and he saluted them as a brave bunch. Tonight's caper could land all of them in the slammer. Only Ira had a compelling personal motive. They turned off the highway and onto a dirt road only wide enough for one vehicle at a time. André broke the silence.

"How much does a bear weigh?" he asked Ira.

"Too much. Seriously, it depends on the bear. Kodiaks tip the scales between twelve hundred and eighteen hundred pounds. The ones that were stolen were the common black bear, or *Ursus americanus*. Ballpark estimate is maybe five hundred pounds or so, less if the animal has been abused."

The van slowed to a stop and the men emerged, to be confronted with a twelve-foot industrial chain-link fence topped with concertina wire. The gate was secured by a heavy chain.

"Well that's that, gentlemen. Let's get out of here." Water dripped from Dennis's nose and over his chin. "It was a good idea, Brian."

"Not so fast." André flashed the beam of his flashlight on the padlock and snorted. "It's always this way. Pay the earth for a security fence and secure the chain with a padlock a baby could open with its teething ring."

Brian's eyes gleamed. "You have this talent?"

"Yeah. I was what you might call a bad boy in high school. Mémé always told me that no knowledge is ever wasted. I guess she was right."

"And who was Mémé, if I may ask?" Dobbs inquired.

"My grandmother."

"A very perspicacious lady," Brian remarked. "Is she still with us?"

"No, she passed away about ten years ago."

"God rest her soul. Let's hope she's looking down on you tonight and is proud. Er, may I hold the light while you work?"

But André was not laying a finger on the tempting padlock. He waved Brian back and shone his own light around the edge of the gate.

"This place is wired. It figures. Father Dennis, do you have a tool kit in the van?"

The kit was produced and the others stood around while André worked. Finally, he gave a grunt of satisfaction. "That does it. You guys, get in the bushes. Father, drive back down the road until you find a good hiding place for the van."

"You do good work." Dobbs looked around for his hiding place. "When will we know if you were successful?"

"Well, either all hell is breaking loose at the police station and at Seward's place or what I did worked. I'd suggest we give it about a half hour before I try my hand on the padlock."

A wet, miserable thirty minutes passed. Thunder rolled overhead. In the intermittent lightning flashes, they strained their eyes for an indication that they had tripped the alarm. Finally, André emerged from his sheltering bush.

"If they're not here by now, I guess we got away with it. Come on, folks." His flashlight shone out and in less than a minute the padlock dangled loose in his hands.

Brian activated his walkie-talkie. "Dennis, do you read me? . . . Good. You stay where you are with the van. We five are going in. If we find what we're looking for, we'll call and guide you in as closely as we can. And we'll check with you every ten minutes to let you know how we're doing."

"I still think it's a wild-goose chase." Ira spoke barely above a whisper. "According to Dobbs there are twenty-five acres to be searched. We don't even know that Seward stole the bears, much less where to start looking."

"Elementary, my dear Grossman," Brian whispered with

more assurance than he felt. "If Seward stole the bears—and how else would he get hold of ursine gall for his mysterious ailment?—he didn't carry them off in his briefcase. They had to have been in a truck or a van and he must have had help. He couldn't have brought them in through the front gates of the estate without risking Audrey's finding out; they had to have come in the back way."

"And they're his big secret," Dobbs added. "He had to hide them somewhere in his half of the estate."

"And lodge them as close to the back entrance as feasible," Brian said, completing Dobbs's thought. "Let's go. Time's a-wastin' and the rain is letting up." He motioned them to wait and he strode in alone.

"What the hell's he doing?" Finbar asked.

Ira chuckled. "Now I get it. I guess the rest of you guys haven't heard of the famous nose. He's trying to smell them out. We follow at a respectful distance."

The faint ammoniac tang of rotted leaves mixed with the mustiness of wet earth. What was G.K. Chesterton's line? "The brilliant smell of water, the brave smell of a stone." A far-off skunk, musky, penetrating. He walked on, pausing every few yards to sniff again. The trouble was that he could be close and miss the place if the wind was in the wrong quarter. Above, the clouds flew across the rapidly clearing sky. Every now and then, they parted enough to let the moon shine on the graveled roadway.

Brian glanced back. The others followed at a distance of about twenty feet, stopping when he stopped. None was using his flashlight; their eyes had adjusted to night vision. These were not children who followed. How long before they decided he was wrong and insisted on turning back?

He was sure he was right about the bears, but he was also afraid they would prove a red herring to the main problem of Abby Meyer's murder. Their abduction might have been the catalyst, though. He raised his head and sniffed again, turning slowly a full 360 degrees.

The irony was that the animals they sought were not endangered, just common black bears that had been taken in and cared for when the mother was injured by a hunter. She and her two cubs became the stars of Delaney's educational program. Schoolkids all over the city adored them. Certainly they had been personally at risk.

Earlier that day Brian had been assigned by Bevilaqua to assist Ira in setting up a breeding-and-nesting site for two pairs of roseate terns that were expected to arrive at the institute in a few days. The species had been listed as endangered since 1987.

As he labored to craft a reasonable facsimile of an offshore island with pebbly beach and wild grassy areas, Ira had filled him in on what he had discovered.

It seemed that Bill McGuire was near retirement from the police department and that he cherished political ambitions. He had categorically refused to let Detective Suarez, the man in charge of the Delaney investigation, compare notes with him on the Abby Meyer murder. He insisted they were two separate matters. According to Joshua, Suarez thought it was because he didn't want to tread on any toes in Abby's rich and powerful family.

Brian stiffened to attention, nose aquiver, as he caught a faint, elusive taint in the air. There it was, the same dark, rancid whiff he'd smelled when Ira took him to the habitat from which the bears had been stolen. Time, water, and fresh air had not been able to completely erase it. Now the same rank odor beckoned him into a small side path with an entrance cannily camouflaged by close-set bushes. He waited until the others joined him.

"This way."

They threaded their way down the narrow path to a small clearing where, behind another high fence, a one-story log hut squatted on the lip of a small pond.

"That's an old icehouse," Dobbs remarked. "See, no windows and only one door." He wrinkled his nose. "What's that god-awful smell?"

Before Brian could tell him, the peace was broken by a menacing growl as a frantic dog hurled itself against the fence.

"I think," said Brian, "that this is a job for Ira."

94

"I love you, too." Ira loaded a tranquilizing dart into his gun. "This poor guy is just doing his duty."

"By God, this is one for the books." Finbar pushed excitedly up to the fence. "That's a pit bull, just the right dog for the job. I'd never have thought that old Leander had it in him."

Ira aimed and shot the dart. The poor dog had time for one infinitely reproachful look, gave a little sigh, and then his legs collapsed beneath him. Ira shone his flashlight over the limp body and shook his head.

"Half-starved and eaten alive with mange. I suppose that bastard Seward thought it would make him more vicious and a better watchdog. Brian, we're taking him along when we leave."

"We'll see." He glanced at his watch. "It's nearly three o'clock. Let's see what's inside the hut."

The hut had no ventilation except the door. The smell Brian had followed through the woods made them gag. They found the bears crammed into three small cages that left them no room to stand or sit erect. They were condemned to crouch all day in their own filth. The half-grown cubs were huddles of misery, barely raising apathetic heads as the men snapped on the overhead lights.

The mother bear was another story. Her lips pulled back in a snarl of hate and her small eyes glowed with madness.

"Stand back, all of you." Brian aimed his camera. I want to get pictures of this, and I don't want any of you guys in them. We're all on the wrong side of the law."

"We're not the criminals," Ira objected.

"Legally, we are." Brian angled his camera to record the full enormity. "I suggest we get the hell out of here and call the Animal Rescue League. We weren't thinking straight. There's no way we could manhandle a full-grown bear and two half-grown ones through that narrow trail, even if they were sedated. I'd like to know how the hell Seward managed it.

"Besides, those cages are set in concrete. Look at them; they were constructed around the animals and have no doors.

How could we get them out without a blowtorch? Sorry, guys. There's nothing I'd have liked better than delivering them back to Delaney, but it's not to be. Ira, take the dog with you after I snap his picture."

17

Deirdre left for Fall River at five in the morning to avoid traffic. By 10:30, she pulled into the parking lot at the Holiday Inn where Maire had told her Brian was staying.

The young man behind the desk tried to be helpful. "He was staying here, Ms. Donodio. I'm sorry, he checked out five days ago."

It helped matters along to be blond, lissome, and gorgeous, with huge blue eyes. Deirdre let the smallest suspicion of a tremble twitch her lower lip. "Did he leave a forwarding address?"

"I'm sorry." The fellow spoke as though he meant it. "Maybe his friend can help you. He's still registered."

"His friend?"

"Yes. A very nice gentleman, Professor Dobbs."

"Is he in?"

"I'll ring his room."

But Dobbs was not in. Deirdre left a message, registered, picked up a copy of the *Herald News,* and went to her room. Nothing like the local paper for getting the lay of the land.

Predictably, the front page was awash with Lizzie Borden stories, mainly rehashes. One small story, below the center fold, was boxed.

STOLEN BEARS FOUND

 The three bears stolen in April from the Delaney Institute were found early today, alive but not well.

 At presstime, the only information received by the *Herald News* was that anonymous information given to the Animal Rescue League and the Barnstable County Sheriff's Office led to an early morning foray into an estate outside Sandwich and to the rescue of the animals that were, in the words of a spokesperson for the league, being "held in abominable conditions."

 The three bears were returned to their quarters at the Delaney Institute School Services Division under the care of Dr. Ira Grossman, D.V.M. Dr. Grossman is the brother of Dr. Liza Borden, the alleged slayer of Abby Meyer.

Deirdre lay back on the bed and closed her eyes. She was pretty sure that Brian's was the fine Italian hand behind the bear caper. Clearly, she needed more information before she called Con to tell him what was going on. And it wouldn't hurt to go out to Delaney and look over the ground. A phone call yielded a recorded message that the institute would open to the public at one o'clock. She set her travel alarm for 12:30 and rolled over to take a nap.

On the drive over to Delaney, she decided to use her married name—much safer, with Brian doing God knows what. Deirdre Connolly, freelance writer, interested in doing a feature story on the institute and the dramatic recovery of the stolen bears. She'd say she hoped to sell the feature to *ZooLife,* a nice conservative glossy magazine with lots of prestige. There was a camera in the trunk of the car and she always carried a notebook.

 She turned her snappy red Volvo in at the gates and smiled at the same teenaged guard who had given Brian a hard time. He gulped and blushed.

 "I'm sorry, Miss. We're not open to the public today."

 Deirdre waved at the TV trucks lined up solidly on each

side of the drive. "But I'm not the public. I'm doing an article for *ZooLife.* If all the other media people can get in, why not me?"

"Well, I don't know." He fished in his TV-addicted brain for some inspiration from the fare on the tube. "Do you have any identification?"

"No." She fixed the blue lasers of her eyes directly on his. "I'm a freelance journalist."

"I gotta check," he mumbled as he turned his back to her and whispered urgently into his walkie-talkie. "What did you say the name of the magazine is?"

"ZooLife."

More muttered colloquy, then he swung open the gate and waved her through. Deirdre pulled to the side, hopped out, and retrieved her camera from the trunk. "Would you mind just standing there by the gate with your radio to your lips?"

"You mean my picture will be in a magazine?" He preened his eyebrows back, settled his cap squarely, and sucked in his gut. "Is this okay?"

What a rat I am, she thought. "Perfect," she said aloud as she clicked her unloaded camera.

"I was told to have you ask for Captain McGuire when you get to the main house. Just follow this road straight around to the parking lot."

Brian sat upright on his power mower, guiding it in careful arcs across the wide lawn. His mind teased away at the problem of Abby's murder. Cui bono? Who benefited? He was totally convinced that the bears were a side issue, though he was delighted that they had been rescued. He was delighted, too, that Leander Seward, that ruiner of a potentially good college, had been snagged along with Dr. Wilbur Chang. Serve them both right. What sort of mind could justify the torture of innocent animals just so he could drain their gallbladders of bile to stiffen his miserable appendage?

Consider O'Hanlon. He stood to gain from Seward's downfall, but not from Delaney's. He hoped to take over

Bowhead and recast it as a first-rate academic institution with emphasis on the earth sciences and the liberal arts. He'd even discussed it with Dobbs and asked whether Dobbs would like to join him. More power to them. But the eagle chicks had been poisoned and O'Hanlon was a world-class toxicologist. . . .

Joshua? The husband or wife was always the first one the police suspected. That didn't fit. Why would Joshua want to kill Abby? She wasn't his wife. Maybe they'd had an affair and she was threatening to tell Liza? Maybe he wanted out from both of his female entanglements? But Joshua had an airtight alibi; he had been at Heritage Park with the boys and several people had seen him there.

The one sure thing was that someone was laughing up his or her sleeve and getting away with murder.

The path of the mower brought him close to the parking area. He watched idly as a bright red Volvo pulled into the lot. Just like Deirdre's. He stiffened as a tall blond woman got out of the car. By God, it was Deirdre! He jerked the mower around and sped off in the other direction.

"Finished already?" Bevilaqua raised an eyebrow as he clattered into the shed.

"I thought I'd take a little break. I've been at it for hours and could use a drink."

"Why not? As long as it's nothing stronger than soda. Why don't you go down and take a look at our returned bears? Everyone else is down there. Dr. Grossman says the cubs are doing okay, but he's not so sure about the mother."

"I'd like to get my hands on the creep."

"We all would. Go along now; there's a lot that needs to be done and I want you back in fifteen minutes. If you see Steve Springer, tell him he's been gawking long enough."

"You're the boss."

"As long as you don't forget it."

"Yes, sir. Mr. Bevilaqua, sir."

He zipped out. He had to warn Ira that Deirdre had arrived. He joined the crowd surrounding the one-way glass partition that had been hastily erected to protect the bears.

100

Oh no. He tried to melt into the crowd of clerks, attendants, and groundspeople who were goggling through the glass while Ira held forth on the abuse, treatment, and prognosis of the bears. It was no use. He was too tall. Deirdre approached, squired on one side by Detective Umberto Suarez and on the other by Capt. Bill McGuire.

Of course McGuire was here. After doing everything he could to impede Suarez's investigation, he was going to snap up the credit. Brian scowled over the heads of the crowd. Deirdre's eyes met his. She didn't bat an eyelash.

Ira was not so restrained. He broke off in the middle of his talk to push his way to her side. "Deirdre! What on earth are you doing here?"

Though he was furious that she was butting in, Brian felt a glow of parental pride at the way she handled Ira.

"Dr. Grossman, imagine your being here. They couldn't have a better person to be in charge of these poor, sweet abused animals. Next time I see my dad, I'll tell him I ran into you. He often speaks of you."

She turned to Suarez and McGuire. "When my old dog was hit by a car, Dr. Grossman performed miracles. You don't know how lucky you are to have him."

Brian backed away inconspicuously.

Once back at the Holiday Inn, he faced a different Deirdre.

"Dad, what the hell do you think you're doing? Before you ask, Mom didn't say a word. She told me you were in Fall River doing garden stuff."

"Who spilled the beans?"

"No one. I put two and two together when I took the dog to see Ira and got an earful from his partner, Dr. Duffy."

Brian lay back on the bed, remembered his filthy sneakers, and sat up to remove them. "I don't want you evicted from the Holiday Inn," he explained.

"Never mind the Holiday Inn, and don't change the subject."

"Where's Con?"

"Working, of course. I have to call him tonight and fill him in."

"So he can call the Fall River cops?"

"It's a possibility."

"No, it is *not*. Sit down, young lady."

"May I remind you that I'm not ten years old anymore? Don't use that tone with me."

"I'm your father. I'll use any tone I like."

An angry red tide was creeping up her neck. She opened her mouth, bit her lip, and plopped down in the chair. She started to laugh.

"What's so funny?"

"We are. We're like a couple of six-year-olds, each trying to prove 'my daddy can lick your daddy.' "

Brian's lips twitched, trembled, and then he broke into a full-throated guffaw. "You're right, I guess we are."

"What's the story?"

Brian told her. He ended by showing her some of the shots of the rescued bears. "The bear rescue is the only positive thing we've done so far, and I'm pretty sure it has nothing to do with the main action. I want you to get ready to come with me to Finbar's house. I have to change out of these work clothes, and I'd like you to meet the Globe Street Irregulars. Then I'll treat you to a decent meal."

"You're on. I'll be ready in a jiffy."

Deirdre was a great hit with Brian's task force who, with the exception of Ira, were all gathered at Finbar's.

"He won't leave his precious bears," Joshua informed them. "I suppose he's right, but I still think he should be with us. After all, Liza is his sister."

"No, I think he's right to stay," André observed. "McGuire might think it odd if he left the animals after all the fuss. Captain Bill doesn't realize there's an ad hoc group paralleling his official investigation."

"Or lack of same," Deirdre observed. "But don't be too

sure that he doesn't realize someone else is nosing around; the man has been a cop for many years.

"Joshua, I know you can think of nothing but Liza right now, but would you mind telling us how you came to be named Borden? Ira told Dad some of the story, but I'd like to hear everything; I'm sure that a big part of the trouble is due to the coincidence of names."

"I'm not a genuine Yankee Borden, as I'm sure you realize. My great-greatgrandfather was an itinerant Eastern European peddler originally named Moses Brodsky. He emigrated to America as a young man. He visited Fall River, liked the town, and made it his home base."

Finbar interrupted. "This sounds like a good yarn. Would anyone like anything before Josh continues? Deirdre?"

"No, thanks. Dad and I are eating out later."

Everyone else refused, so Joshua took up the tale again. "Well, in a nutshell, Andrew Jackson Borden—he's the one Lizzie allegedly axed—met Moses and offered him a job, not realizing that his name had been changed to Borden by the immigration people in Boston."

Dobbs interrupted. "But surely . . ."

"There had been Bordens around this area since 1635, when a John Borden arrived from England. They had obeyed the Biblical injunction to increase and multiply with great zeal. No one knew all the distant cousins. John Borden had been exiled by the Massachusetts Bay Company because he was a follower of Anne Hutchinson. He settled in Portsmouth. His grandson, Richard Borden, settled an argument by buying the water rights in what is now the Fall River area and they became a powerful family.

"The power and the glory continued until the family mantle was assumed by Andrew Borden's father, Abraham, who was a lousy businessman. He lost everything except the water rights. Those, and a broken-down cottage on Ferry Street, were his legacy to Andrew, who developed into an acute businessman and, by all accounts, an unsavory person.

"One of the things he tried was undertaking. It's rumored that he was not above shortening the legs of the loved ones to save on lumber. However, he did restore the family fortune and was able to offer Moses a job."

"Then Moses was around when he got axed?" Finbar leaned forward, his face alight with interest.

"He sure was. In fact, let me tell you something that only we Brodskys know. Do you remember the mysterious letter Emma Borden, Lizzie's sister, got from a man who identified himself as Samuel Robinsky, a Jewish peddler?"

"I remember. Wasn't he the one who claimed to have seen a man covered with blood on the road to New Bedford on the day the Bordens were axed?"

"That's the one. Emma was reported to have been amused by his letter. Well, there's a family tradition that the writer of the letter was Moses Brodsky. He was very fond of Lizzie Borden, used to say that she was the only one in the family worth a damn, and he wrote the letter to take the heat off her. Of course, we have no proof."

"So, what's the moral of this cautionary tale?" Brian asked.

"Hang on to your water rights. Don't forget, Moses Brodsky arrived in Fall River around 1880. Things were a lot looser then and there was no Social Security.

"It was tough being an Eastern European Jew in New England. Brodsky let Borden go right on being mistaken and he registered his children as Borden on their birth certificates, but never in the family's private records."

"Didn't his accent raise a few eyebrows?" Deirdre inquired.

"He had a genius for language. By the time he arrived in Fall river, he spoke English like a Yankee."

André had a thing about ethnic heritage; it showed in his voice. "If I were you, the first thing I'd have done when I came of age was change my name back legally."

"If only I had, but I always thought it was a good joke. Liza wanted us to change. If I'd listened to her, Abby might still be alive and my wife wouldn't be in jail."

"Thanks for a good story." Brian looked at his watch. "It's nearly eight o'clock and I'm starving. Come along, daughter."

They took Deirdre's car across the Brightman Street Bridge to a small restaurant in Somerset where, Dennis had told them, the food was outstanding. It was housed in a Federal mansion on Riverside Avenue which overlooked the water. The ground floor had been gutted into one huge room that opened onto a deck for alfresco dining in the summer. Across the river, the lights of Fall River reflected from the surface of the water.

Brian felt like a kid with an unexpected free day from school. He was getting sick of his masquerade as a grubby has-been and of speaking like an ignoramus. Damn it, he enjoyed going out with his beautiful daughter, wearing a decent suit, and feeling clean.

"I like the beard." Deirdre raised her glass. "Here's to us."

"Exactly what does that mean?" He touched her glass of ginger ale with his libation of single malt.

"That I'm with you on this one. You guys are doing a great job, but you need me."

"I'll drink to that. What are you planning to do for us?"

"Let's eat and then talk. I'm starving."

They agreed on St. Germain soup, that delectable blend of marrowfat peas and spices excelled in by French-Canadian cooks, followed by lobster à la béchamel, then crowned it all off with large dishes of Indian pudding topped with whipped cream.

"This is a sin."

"A pleasant one. I've been eating at greasy spoons for breakfast, brown-bagging it for lunch, and having nouvelle cuisine dinners with Finbar and André for a week. How much is a man supposed to take? I miss your mother. How do you think she'll feel about the beard?"

"I wouldn't presume to guess. That's a husband-and-wife question."

He ordered a liqueur, settled back, and eased his belt. "Now, what did you mean when you said, 'I'm with you on this one'?"

"Does anyone in your gang have access to a computer?"

"I guess they all use them one way or another. If you're asking if anyone is a serious hacker, I doubt it."

She glanced at her watch. "Time to go."

"Where are we going?"

"To see a friend of mine who works at Bridgewater State College."

"Isn't it late to go calling?"

"He's a night owl. I called him and he's expecting us. I'll tell you about him on the way." Deirdre steered the Volvo out of the lot and they headed back across the river. "José Abarca is from Colombia. He's a darling guy and a real genius with computers; they're his passion. When I was with the INS I was able to help him, and I found a sponsor for Rosa—that's his wife. I was able to get him and his family into the country legally, so he thinks he owes me. I'm going to call in my markers."

"You never cease to amaze me."

"You're the one who's going to be amazed when you find out how little real privacy we have once a dedicated hacker gets to work."

He snorted. "I found out about that sort of thing on the Maureen Sullivan case."

In about thirty minutes they drew up in front of a nondescript ranch house of the type that proliferated just after World War II. When Deirdre cut the motor, the front door of the house flew open. A man and woman, followed by two little boys and three dogs, emerged.

"José and Rosa, it's good to see you."

"Come in; come in. We have been waiting."

The man was short and heavyset. Dark brown eyes flashed from under bushy brows. His beaming smile revealed a set of flashing teeth surmounted by a Che Guevara mustache. He spoke with only a slight accent, but his stiff formalism and lack of idiom showed that he was not a native speaker.

Rosa stood shyly beside him. She was very tiny and was obviously about to present the world with a third little Abarca in the near future. Her broad features, high cheekbones, and straight black hair revealed her indigenous Colombian heritage. She held the little fellows by the hands as Brian and Deirdre stepped inside.

"Rosa, I would like to present my father, Dr. Brian Donodio. Dad, this is Rosa Abarca and her husband, José."

"An honor, Mrs. Abarca." Brian raised her hand to his lips. "A pleasure, Mr. Abarca."

"The honor is ours, Dr. Donodio. My family owes yours a debt that can never be repaid. May I present our sons, Pedro and Luis."

Luis, the elder, shook hands with aplomb. Pedro, still a toddler, slid behind his mother's skirt and regarded Brian with a solemn unwinking gaze. The three dogs sniffed, judged, then settled down.

The Abarca living room was small and spotlessly clean. A well-worn couch and easy chair, probably Salvation Army or Goodwill in origin, stood on the linoleum tile floor. Bookcases built of bricks and boards covered one wall and wooden packing cases, sanded and stained, served as end tables and supports for dime-store lamps.

The only object of beauty was a glowing tapestry worked in earth tones with green, red, violet, and blue accents that dominated the room. It depicted a great tree sheltering children and animals in its branches. The tree stood in a flowering field and it sprang from an archetypal female figure. Deirdre was spellbound.

"It's very beautiful."

José beamed. "My Rosa made it. It is the tree of life and it shows how all things reach to heaven."

"Rosa did this?"

"Yes. It is the only one she was able to bring with her from Colombia."

Brian knew that Maire would flip her lid over such hangings in her decorating business. "Does she ever think of making them professionally?"

José made a dismissive gesture. "Now she is too busy. Her work is with the children and the house. Many women in my country amuse themselves with such things. But please, I

107

forget my manners. Be seated and may I offer you some refreshment?"

Deirdre knew that to refuse was an insult. "We just finished dinner, but later we would be very happy to have a soda or some coffee. José, we need your help. Do you still have your computer setup in the basement?"

"Of course, and I have an even better setup at the college. What is it that you need me to do?"

"We need to know anything and everything you can find out about the following people and institutions. Here, I made a list."

The list read:

Finbar Duane O'Hanlon
Abigail Meyer
Joshua Borden
Capt. William McGuire, FRPD
Detective Umberto Suarez, FRPD
Rebecca Betancourt Delgado, Esq.
Reverend Dennis Duque
Leander Seward, D.Ed.
Audrey MacTavish Seward
Bowhead College
Meyer the Builder, Inc.
Rep. Susan Meyer
The Delaney Institute

18

REBECCA BETANCOURT DELGADO was a genius at pulling strings. Not even Joshua could get in to see Liza before her case went to the grand jury, but Brian had been granted a second interview as a member of Rebecca's staff. It was set for ten o'clock Sunday morning. Bill McGuire had urged the judge at the bail hearing to send her for psychiatric evaluation. So far, Rebecca had managed to block him. Liza was still being held in the Dartmouth facility, where Brian had interviewed her the last time. After early Mass, he drove to Dartmouth, primed with a list of what Deirdre considered vital questions.

If anything, Liza looked worse than before. Surely he would have noticed the gray strands streaking her hair if they had been there on his last visit. Last time, he'd noticed how slender she was. This time, there were black shadows under her eyes and he could see the shape of her skull. He rose to his feet as she approached.

"Joshua sends his love and so do the boys. Ira is filling in for you at Delaney and we have found the bears. That's all the good news. If we had time, I'd tell you all about it, but we have only ten minutes and there are questions I have to ask you." He glanced at his watch.

Her expression lightened at his news, but she accepted the need for economy. "Go ahead. I'll do the best I can."

"What happens to Delaney if the board or the trustees decide that all the problems make it impossible to carry on? Or if they feel that the institute is not fulfilling its mandate to study and conserve endangered species?"

"It was explained to me that the board and the trustees have the power to close down the institute."

"Who gets the money and the assets?"

"There are cousins who are kin to Jack Delaney. They tried to challenge Mrs. Delaney's will, but they lost the case."

"Who are they?"

"I don't know. It was all settled before I got there."

Brian made a note. "Okay. Now, who on the board is gung ho about getting to the bottom of the problems?"

"Abby was, Finbar, and myself. I got the feeling that Caspar Lovelace was on our side. He's a nonvoting member of the board."

"Who is he?"

"He's the trustee for the Delaney estate and its lawyer. He's the institute's lawyer as well, and very closemouthed. The idea was to coordinate both bodies through him."

"I guess that makes sense."

"And there's Verity Fletcher; she's the treasurer. And Pierre Bouchard is the secretary."

Brian's yellow pad was filling up rapidly. "Tell me about them."

She tugged on her left ear, a mannerism he suddenly remembered from her student days. It meant she thought the questions being asked were silly and a waste of time. "Surely Joshua and Finbar have told you all this."

"We've gone over it, but I want to hear about them from your point of view. Just pretend that I know nothing."

She sighed. "Oh, all right. It wasn't that Fletcher, Lovelace, and Bouchard were pushing to close down the place. It just was that they seemed so cautious about doing anything positive. Bill McGuire was a little different. His position was that he had to keep his job as a policeman separate from his job as chairman. I can understand that."

She pushed her limp hair back from her forehead and tears

110

came into her eyes. "I'm sorry, I'm just so scared. And McGuire keeps talking about sending me for psychiatric evaluation. That would mean Bridgewater, and it's an awful place. Did you see that documentary on PBS? The one that was kept off the air by political influence for twenty-five years?"

He'd seen it and didn't blame her for being terrified if she thought she'd be sent to Bridgewater, but hadn't anyone explained to her? "Who threatened you with Bridgewater? McGuire? Didn't anyone tell you that only men are confined there?"

The tears she'd been blinking back started to pour down her cheeks and her whole body shook. "Are you telling me the truth?"

"Of course I am. Did McGuire tell you he'd send you there?"

"Not specifically. He just kept talking about psychiatrists and facilities for the criminally insane, and I assumed . . ."

"How about Rebecca? Didn't you tell her how you felt?"

A rueful half smile touched her lips. "I never talked about it. Tried to play it cool, I guess. I didn't want her to think I was a coward. It probably never occurred to her that I didn't know they couldn't send me to Bridgewater."

"Well, now you know."

"I kept wanting to die." She sniffed and dabbed at her nose. "Not that I'd do anything foolish." She raised an eyebrow and shrugged. "We Jews are like Timex watches—'take a licking and keep on ticking.' I'm so worried about Joshua and the boys."

"The boys are fine and Joshua is holding up well. The best chance you have lies in our proving who really killed Abby. I have an idea, but I'm a long way from proving it and I need all the help I can get. Now, tell me about Verity Fletcher."

"Sorry." She shivered and straightened her slumped shoulders. "Verity—about sixty, never married, old Yankee family, the genuine article. Lives off the loot that generations of Fletchers stashed away in the State Street Bank, probably from the Triangular Trade.

"Tweed skirts, cashmere sweaters, real pearls, hats, flat

heels—she buys good stuff and wears it for years. You know the type?"

"I know the type." He checked the time. "Do you think she's honest?"

"Rigidly. Pillar of the Congregational Church. She's one of those people who divides humanity into us and them and doesn't quite know what to do with people who don't conform. She's charitable to the less fortunate sectors of society, but they have to be deserving and know their place." A little color started to creep into her cheeks and animation into her voice. He remembered that she had starred in creative writing in school as well as in science. It was a tonic for her to give these verbal portraits. He could almost see the lady being described.

"She missed her right time in history. In the eighteenth century, she'd have made a smashing lady of the manor."

"We have only a minute to go. Quick, tell me about Bouchard."

"He's harmless. Runs an insurance agency and follows McGuire's lead. He was put on the board so the French community wouldn't feel slighted. He's a whiz at raising money."

"Then he's very valuable and not harmless at all."

The corrections officer rose and took her by the arm.

"Oh, oh, time's up. I wish I could hug you. I'll tell Joshua you're holding up well and send your love." She was almost out the door. "Keep your chin up." The door slammed shut on her sad little wave.

He made a beeline for a pay phone to call Deirdre. "Hi, sweetheart. Call José and add these names to his list: Caspar Lovelace, Verity Fletcher, and Pierre Bouchard."

Action time. It was still only 10:20 A.M. Brian spared a wistful thought for Deirdre's snappy red Volvo as he backed his Chevy out of the North Dartmouth parking lot. Where to go first? It was a fairly safe bet that Verity Fletcher would be doing the Congregational thing and that McGuire, that pillar of St. Fiacre's, was at the 10:30 Mass. A quick peek at the parish schedule in Dennis's office had listed him as the lector this morning. Maybe he could take a quick look around McGuire's office at Delaney before they opened to the public at one o'clock.

No, that was no good. If anyone saw him, there went his cover as Brian the groundsman. He couldn't contact Caspar Lovelace. His office was in Boston and he did not have the man's home address. He made a mental note for Ira to dig it out of the files.

Discussions with the Globe Street Irregulars were getting tedious. It was time to break new ground.

From Liza, he had gleaned that Verity Fletcher's stamping ground was the First Congregational Church on Rock Street. He parked down the block and approached the large Gothic Revival building.

Liza had described Verity as Yankee to her fingertips and very fond of hats. From the back pew where he crouched, Brian surveyed the worshipers. There was a fine hat in the front pew, an autumnal one of russet felt, wide-brimmed and garnished with the plumage of an unfortunate pheasant. In tribute to true Yankee thrift, the hat had seen many seasons. One wing was spread in a sweeping curve down the wearer's neck, almost brushing squared shoulders and the top of a ramrod spine adorned with a set of fox furs. The kind his grandmother used to wear: beady glass eyes, dangling paws, and a mouth operated by a spring so the jaw of the first fox clamped firmly to the tail of the ultimate animal.

The service was nearly over. After the final blessing, the organ surged into the opening bars of "Blest Be the Tie That Binds." He rose to his feet, singing lustily.

How to approach Verity if, indeed, it was she? He nipped smartly into the aisle just ahead of the pheasant hat and joined the line waiting to shake hands with the minister, a large amiable-looking fellow who smiled at his flock and had a word for each. He reached the front of the line.

"Welcome to the stranger within our gates." Brian's hand was pumped with enthusiasm.

113

" 'If a man be gracious and courteous to strangers, it shows he is a citizen of the world.' Bacon."

"Thrice welcome to a literate stranger. May I inquire your name?"

"Donodio. Brian Donodio." He glanced over his shoulder expectantly.

"Mr. Donodio, may I present one of the mainstays of our worshiping community, Miss Verity Fletcher."

"A pleasure, Miss Fletcher."

"Will you join us for coffee?" A faint whiff of camphor from the fur piece and the pheasant, mixed with castile soap and talcum powder, drifted up to tickle Brian's nose.

Bull's-eye! "I would be delighted, Miss Fletcher. I hope to see you later, Reverend." They moved away together. Now that he could see her face he realized he had seen her around Delaney, though they had never spoken. He prayed she had not recognized him.

"Here, try one of the brownies. I baked them myself."

"Thank you. They look delicious."

"And so do you, Mr. Donodio. Much better than you do in your MacMorrough persona. I've had my eye on you." The eye in question glittered shrewdly.

"Hoist by my own petard. Look, I can explain. I came here this morning to have a word with you."

"Go ahead. Which name is correct? Or are they both false?"

"Both my own. I'm Brian MacMorrough Donodio."

She planted her feet firmly in their Sunday-best court heels and prepared to listen. No one seemed to be paying any attention and, judging by the cut of Verity's jib, Liza had made an accurate assessment of her character. He told her everything.

114

19

It was a rapturous reunion. Had it only been two days? Deirdre and Con, as was right and proper, occupied their first couple of hours in a nonverbal means of communication. First things first.

When they finally flagged from assuring each other that each was intact with all moving parts in working order, Con propped himself up on his elbow.

"Now, what's going on with Brian? I figured there was a reason for your urgent message on the tape telling me not to contact the Fall River Police Department. I tried to call back a couple of times, but you were out."

"I know you did. I got the messages, but I decided to wait until I could lay the whole thing out for you." She hopped out of bed and went to the desk. "I've got a lot of stuff to show you."

"I'll say you have." He came up behind and caught her round the waist. "You'd better put something on or I'll be looking at the wrong things."

"You sound positively uxorious."

"And who has a better right?"

"Wouldn't you like to know?" She reached behind. "Ah, *bene pependit.*"

"If that means what I think it means . . ."

"It means you have a wife who's a credit to her education. I can talk dirty in Latin."

"Aha, a multiculturalist."

"If you say so." She freed herself and pulled on her robe. "Look at this stuff, starting with the pictures."

Half an hour later, he looked up from the last of her notes. "So?"

"Do you realize that Liza Borden used to baby-sit me occasionally when she went to the Prendergast School and that she's being framed? I told Dad that I'm helping him on this one. There's no danger either to him or to me, or anyone else for that matter. Whoever did it, he or she can't murder anyone else. It would destroy the frame against Liza."

There was a long silence as he considered her statement. "I don't agree. I can think of several ways to do it without rousing suspicion of anything but an accident. If it's who you think it is, you and Brian had better tread very softly."

20

BRIAN AND VERITY Fletcher sat back and relaxed after an excellent lunch at her house in Somerset overlooking the river. He sighed with contentment and declaimed:

> *Flowers in the garden, meat in the hall,*
> *A bin of wine, a spice of wit,*
> *A house with lawns enclosing it,*
> *A living river by the door,*
> *A nightingale in the sycamore!*

"I see you know your Stevenson; you can't be all bad," Verity remarked. "Of course you know that the nightingale is not native to the Americas. Aside from that one inaccuracy, I take the quotation as a compliment to my home and my company. Now, Dr. Donodio, you have told me a rather unbelievable story, but, for some reason, I believe it. Not that I approve of your methods. Mendacious actions are as bad as verbal untruths, and you have been passing yourself off as something you are not. Be that as it may, I do not for one minute think that Liza Borden is guilty. How may I help you?"

"Several ways." He surveyed the low-ceilinged living room with pleasure, noting the wide-board floors and the paneling around the fireplace. "I'm admiring your home. It reminds me of my own place in New York, even though mine is Dutch-Colonial in origin and yours is New England. How old is the original part of the house?"

"There have been Fletchers living here since 1699. Later, if you're interested, I'll show you a diary kept by my ancestor Dorcas Fletcher. She recorded the first winter when they lived in the roofed-over hole that is now the cellar. Unfortunately, when I go, there will be no one left carrying the name except some distant cousins in Hawaii."

"I'd be honored to see Mistress Fletcher's diary. Hawaii?"

"Yes. Fletchers were among the early settlers from New England. They no longer call themselves Yankees. I believe the native Hawaiian word for them is *haoles*. I went there to visit once, but I felt like a fish out of water. All string bikinis and luaus. Now, to the subject at hand."

"Indeed. First, would you mind telling me how you recognized me?"

"I taught adolescent girls for forty years. It sharpens one's powers of observation. Your grounds work was too meticulous for an itinerant laborer who gave the impression that he looked upon the wine when it was red."

"Anything else?"

"You were not consistent in your mangling of the English language."

"Go on."

"Once, when I was in my office with the window open and you were clipping the hedge under the window, I heard you whistling Mozart's "Alleluia." Now, any one of these things might be explainable. All of them together aroused my suspicions."

"Did you voice those suspicions?"

"I did ask Mr. Bevilaqua what he knew about you. He referred me to Finbar O'Hanlon."

"And what did Finbar tell you?"

"That you were a queer duck but a good worker—the same things he told the board when he suggested we hire you. With that, I had to be satisfied."

"How about Bill McGuire? Did you say anything to him?"

She snorted. "That pompous, bigoted, self-satisfied wind-bag! I wouldn't give him the time of day."

"Which brings us to your work for Delaney. I know, and you have told me you believe, Liza to be an innocent victim. Are you willing to tell me about the finances of the institute?"

"Who scoops the pot if we go down the tubes, to mix my metaphors?"

"Precisely."

She stirred restlessly. "It's hard to say. I can speak generally, but I don't know about specifics. I do know that I wouldn't mind being old Delaney's closest kin." She got up and took a leash down from its hook by the door. "I usually take a walk with my dog after lunch on Sunday. Would you like to accompany me? Somerset is a very pleasant place."

He rose with alacrity.

Riverside Avenue led past a small marina and shipyard to the entrance of a park opposite a white-painted Georgian church. They sat on a bench overlooking the water, with the dog, an ancient clumber spaniel, panting at their feet.

Brian surveyed the two well-equipped empty play-grounds. They looked very inviting in the afternoon sunshine. "I would think those would be crowded with youngsters on a fine day like this."

"They will be in a short while. Everyone is at home eating their Sunday dinners."

"So, who is the closest living Delaney kin?"

"Good question. I don't know. Some of the cousins tried to contest her will, but I don't know if they were actually the closest relatives. The suit was filed before I became treasurer and I didn't pay much attention to the details. I do know that Finbar O'Hanlon was involved.

"Rumor has it that Mr. Delaney kept Mrs. Delaney in the mansion and a couple of other types of ladies down on Bedford Street in a less luxurious fashion. Rumor also has it that there were by-blows, if you know what I mean."

"They'd be rather long in the tooth by now."

"But their children would be only in late middle age."

"And their grandchildren in the prime of lusty youth. Tell me about Abby Meyer's family. Everyone is concentrating on Liza Borden, but you don't hear about Abby's people."

Verity sighed and shifted on the bench. "I was quite fond of Abby. She had a very poor education at Bowhead College, but she didn't have a nasty bone in her body. She was the type who got carried away by causes. Everyone's real or imagined grievance became a crusade until the next thing came along."

"What about her parents?"

"Bernard Meyer is a very successful businessman. Republican, of course. I was one myself until that motley crew of actors and crooks took over the country. The whole board attended Abby's funeral. I'm ashamed to say that it was the first time I've ever been in a synagogue. Abby's uncle sang a beautiful prayer in Hebrew. It brought tears to my eyes."

"It's called the Kaddish."

"She was the only child of Bernard Meyer's first marriage. Abby told me once that her mother was not Jewish by birth. After her death, Abby's father married a young woman who promptly presented him with three strapping sons and two more daughters. One of the boys told me that the family does not believe for one minute that Liza killed Abby. He says they were like sisters. In fact, it was Bernard Meyer who sent his own lawyer to help Liza."

Brian chuckled as he made a note. "Have you met Ms. Rebecca Betancourt Delgado, Esq.?"

"Only seen her on the tube. I asked Caspar Lovelace about her."

"What was his report?"

"Top of her class at New York University Law School, editor of the review, clerked for Justice Marshall, visiting lecturer at Harvard Law, three books on criminal jurisprudence, and she argued and won a landmark decision before the Supreme Court. In other words, a good woman to have on one's side."

He glanced at his watch. "It's getting late and I don't want to keep you, delightful though this is. Three more things come to mind. As treasurer, have you noticed anyone trying to pull any shenanigans with the money?"

Verity's mouth tightened with outraged Yankee probity. "They'd better not. Mrs. Delaney's will made provision for setting up and equipping the institute. In order to keep it running, we have to raise money, and her estate matches every dollar we raise. If we don't raise enough, we're goners."

"How have you done so far?"

"The problem is that the donations fell off when the word got around about the bears, the poisoned eaglets, and the other mutilated animals. The less we raise, the less we get in matching funds. Now, with this thing about Liza generating such bad publicity, donations are nil."

"Then, if I understand the terms of the will, the money and property revert to the next of kin."

"Precisely." She snapped off the word with a click of her dentures.

"And how is Bill McGuire handling it? I gather he's not your favorite person."

"He's spending every available penny to increase security. It's like working on a military base; you know that. The more we spend on security, the less we have for research and our real purpose, and that will shut us down even faster." She shrugged. "I suppose I have to expect a policeman to approach the problem like a policeman."

"One last question, and this has nothing to do with anything." He pointed up the hill. "What are those huge orange pipes snaking down the hillside?"

Her eyes shone. "Those, Dr. Donodio, are slides—covered plastic pipes with slick interiors. A child climbs in at the top and whooshes down to the bottom to land with a bump."

"Have you ever tried them?"

"I've been tempted but . . . no. What would people think?"

He caught her hand. "No one's here to think anything. Grab the dog and let's go."

The plastic pipes were a blast. They zoomed down again and again, stopping only when a gaggle of youngsters arrived and joined the lineup. Brian was willing to take his turn with the kids, but Verity blushed to her hairline.

"I'll be the talk of the neighborhood." She untied the dog. He'd been very upset each time his mistress vanished into the orange maw, raising his gray muzzle and giving voice to heartbreaking ululations.

"So what if you are? Are the kids the only ones allowed to have fun in Somerset?" He pushed his glasses up on the bridge of his nose and rescued his fedora from its perch on a handy bush. "Let's go back to the house. Would you trust me with Caspar Lovelace's home number?"

Her eyes gleamed in a way that made him uneasy. She cooed, "I'd trust you with everything."

"Not everything," he said hastily. "Just the number will be fine."

Now he was on his way to Boston. A call from Somerset brought the information that Lovelace was, indeed, at home and would be more than happy to speak with Dr. Donodio. Any friend of Verity's . . .

Lovelace lived on Acorn Street, a block-long byway on Beacon Hill still paved with nineteenth-century cobblestones. His house was a three-story redbrick Federal with a green door, green shutters, and window boxes sporting white mums and trailing ivy. Electrified gas lights illumined the uneven brick sidewalks. Lovelace himself answered the door.

Brian instantly categorized him as *Homo superioris,* genus vespa, nor was he being snide. The man looked like a very good example of the species: tall, sparely built, with his long Yankee jaw and narrow lips softened by laugh lines running from his straight nose to his chin. Wrinkles radiated out from the corners of his blue eyes as if he spent a lot of time out of doors, gazing into the distance. Maybe a sailor? His glance met Brian's squarely; his handshake was firm and dry. His prevailing aroma was Ivory Soap and bay rum.

"Dr. Donodio, come in. You had no trouble finding the place?"

"None whatsoever. I even found a parking space just around the corner."

"Beginner's luck."

The entrance hall was floored in black-and-white marble and centered with a threadbare Oriental rug. In dramatic contrast to the traditional architecture, a Helen Frankenthaler original dominated one wall, its overlapping squares and tall rectangles drawing the eye to unimaginable distances. Lovelace followed his glance.

"I like the contrast with the hall and I never tire of looking into that picture."

"I see what you mean. It's a thing to live with."

"Let's go into the library, where we can talk."

When they were settled with glasses of single malt in front of the fire, Brian leaned back in the leather armchair to study the seascape over the mantel. "Winslow Homer?"

"You have a good eye. I collect American paintings. Now, Verity told me you are here about the Liza Borden accusation and the Delaney Institute. Terrible business, just terrible. How may I help?"

"I understand that you're on the board of Delaney and also the lawyer for the Delaney estate."

"That's right."

"No conflict of interest?"

"None that I can see. We're not adversaries. Of course, I'm a nonvoting member—advice but no consent. It's my business to see that the terms of Mrs. Delaney's will are carried out by the institute. In legalese, I'm the fiduciary. I've been given a very wide mandate. Did Verity tell you that Mrs. Delaney was my aunt?"

"No, she didn't. Doesn't *that* cause a conflict of interest? I understand that if the institute fails in its purpose, the estate passes to the next of kin."

"You're only half right. Nothing goes to Aunt Emily's next of kin. It all goes to Jack Delaney's side, as is only fair. After all, he's the one who made the money.

"Of course I know many of them; they're family. Finbar O'Hanlon's mother was Jack Delaney's cousin. There's a huge

123

Delaney tribe in New Bedford. Jack's grandfather was a very busy man; there are second and third cousins scattered all the way from County Antrim to Calcutta. I want to show you something."

He took a large album from one of the lower shelves and turned to a group picture. "Two years ago we organized a Delaney family reunion. This is everyone who was able to come. For everyone who showed up, there are half a dozen others at home."

Brian gazed in awe. The panoramic shot showed a couple of hundred people standing in ranks, with a crowd of children cross-legged on the ground in front. "My God, is this all one family?"

"And then some. I have nightmares about the distribution if the foundation goes under."

"I can see why."

"There's another wrinkle. My aunt Emily was one of the fairest and most forgiving women I ever met. I don't know how she put up with Jack all those years. She was a very old-fashioned lady with strong convictions about 'till death do us part.' Stiff-backed, never moaned about her troubles. She couldn't have children and she was very upset about the harm to the environment caused by industry. Jack's factories were major offenders."

"Hence the institute?"

"Precisely. She was very practical, though. She didn't just leave her money outright to give the institute a free ride."

"Verity explained to me about the matching funds."

"Well, to make a long story short, Aunt Emily knew all about Jack's sins and the results of them. When she knew she hadn't long to go, she gave me an envelope that was to be opened only if the institute didn't work out. My guess is that it contains the names of Jack's direct descendants. By now, it would be mainly his grandchildren on the other side of the blanket. Only a guess, mind. I've never opened that envelope, and I won't unless Delaney goes under."

"Of course not," Brian agreed. "But what a motive."

"Don't you think I haven't thought of that? And framing

Liza Borden was the final blow. That young woman is no more a murderer than I am."

"Have you discussed it with McGuire?"

"Until I'm blue in the face. He insists that the two cases are not connected, that there's no evidence."

"One final question. Just as a ballpark estimate, how much money are we talking about?"

"Real estate, stocks, bonds, and so on, I'd say about fifty million."

21

DEIRDRE SAT CROSS-LEGGED on the bed, surrounded by computer printouts. "Here's everything you don't want to know about everybody. I'm tempted to have José go back into the data banks and erase all the Donodio and Connolly records. Talk about lack of privacy."

Con shifted uneasily in his chair. "You realize that this is totally illegal?"

"Any Tom, Dick, or Harry with the know-how can tap into everyone's personal affairs. Why should we be any different? What's illegal is axing Abby Meyer and framing Liza."

Brian flipped over a stack of paper. "Con, if your conscience is bothering you, why don't you go out and get us something to eat?"

"My conscience is fine. I just want to be sure you understand that none of this stuff can be used as evidence."

"Understood. Let's get to work. I think some of these people may be dismissed out of hand. Verity Fletcher, for instance. Net worth about three million, all of it conservatively invested. Tax records, immaculate. The woman has no credit cards, no charge accounts, no unpaid bills, no outstanding mortgages. Supports the Congregational Church, the United Negro College Fund, the United Way, Amnesty International,

Oxfam, and the Sierra Club. Verity, I'm proud to know you."

Deirdre looked up from her sorting. "Quite a few like that. Here"—she handed over a neat stack—"look at these for starters."

"Abigail Meyer." Brian jotted a note on his trusty yellow pad. "Nothing leaps out. She was doing quite well in real estate until the recent slump. A bit of a cash-flow problem, but still a comfortable income. No major debts. Her mother's maiden name was O'Connor. I can't see anything here."

"Nor can I," she answered. "I just wanted to be able to eliminate a financial motive for her murder. Now look at this one."

"Finbar. He's a full professor at Bowhead and his nursery business is doing well. He has the royalty income from several books and he lectures a lot. He should be sitting pretty."

She passed over another sheet. "He isn't. He's behind on his mortgage payments, his credit cards are charged to the limit, and José couldn't find any trace of savings or investments."

"Let me see." Con reached for the sheets. "You said this guy's gay? Blackmail?"

Brian shook his head. "I don't think so. He's openly gay and it's not illegal. He obviously needs money, though. He's been talking to Dobbs about some scheme to take over Bowhead College, and Verity and Caspar told me he's related to the Delaneys. Put him aside on the 'maybe' pile."

"The Sewards?"

"No. I'm pretty sure their connection is peripheral. And I'm sure his little caper with the bears cooked his goose for good with the trustees of Bowhead. Finbar told me that they've called a special meeting for tomorrow and the skinny is that they're calling for his resignation and turning down Audrey's bequest. How about André St. Cyr?"

"He wasn't on our original list, but I called José and added his name," Deirdre said. "Nothing. Finbar pays him a reasonable salary and he's co-owner of their house. As far as I can tell, he's just Finbar's significant other."

"I'd like to have a talk with Abby's father. Verity told me

today that he's the one who arranged for Rebecca to act as Liza's attorney."

"You wouldn't be welcome, Dad. The family's through sitting shivah, but they're still in mourning and Mr. Meyer has not yet returned to his office. They've hired guards to protect their privacy. I can't see anything out of line on Mr. Meyer's records or his sister's, the one at the State House."

"Which brings us to the brave boys in blue, Suarez and McGuire."

Con grabbed the two printouts. "Let me; I'm the expert on cops." He laid the two sheets side by side. His lips pursed in a soundless whistle. "Well, well, well."

"What have you got?" Deirdre and Brian spoke in chorus.

"Suarez is making regular cash deposits to a savings account that are too large to come out of his salary, unless Fall River is the only city in the country paying their police what they're worth. Judging from his credit cards and his taste in cars, he's a young man with very expensive tastes. Not married. I'd say he should be looked at by Internal Affairs or whatever they call it in this neck of the woods."

"And McGuire?"

"Didn't you say he has political ambitions?"

"That's the general opinion."

"Well, I think he got his first political lesson down pat. Hide the loot. His financial situation seems unexceptionable." He paused dramatically, "Except . . ."

"Except what?" Brian demanded.

"Why should he need accounts in the Cayman Islands and in Switzerland?"

Deirdre looked wise. "Drugs, protection, payoffs, blackmail, you name it. No one seems to like him."

"Be fair," Brian interjected. "The general consensus seems to be that the man is stupid and pigheaded, not evil. He's head of the parish council at St. Fiacre's, a lector, and a Eucharistic minister. Dennis tells me that he's a devoted husband and grandfather. Maybe he got an inheritance or a big win in the lottery and is just trying to avoid some taxes. I'd fault no man for that."

Con raised his eyebrows. "Maybe," he conceded, but he didn't sound convinced.

Deirdre waved another paper. "Here's Father Duque."

"You look at it, Con. I've known Dennis since we were kids. He officiated at my wedding and I just cannot invade his privacy like this. The Duque family was pretty well heeled, as I recall. He was their only child, so he should have come in for something substantial when they passed away. It probably all went to the Sulpicians. Order priests take a vow of poverty."

Con read in silence, then reached out to grab one of the sheets he had already considered. "I can't see anything here to connect Father Duque with Abby, Liza, or Delaney. I'm pretty sure of one thing, though."

"And that is?"

"Your Father Duque is being blackmailed and the money he's paying out matches the mysterious deposits to Umberto Suarez's savings account."

"I don't have to be back at work until Tuesday." Con took a huge bite of his *chourico* sandwich and regarded Deirdre and Brian with a dreamy expression. "Do they sell this sausage in New York?"

"Probably at Zabar's, and it would cost a week's pay. I'll buy some to take home before we leave. Shush and let me eat." Deirdre had no time for table chat.

The Uke was a success with Con and Deirdre, but Brian did not wish to linger; the night was still fairly young and he had other fish to fry. He gulped down his last bite, wiped his lips, and rose.

"I'll leave you two to savor the delights of Fall River." He threw some bills on the table. "Take care of things, will you?"

"Where are you going?"

"Here and there. Back and forth."

Deirdre added, "And up and down, I suppose? I don't trust you."

"When did you ever? All right, I'm going to pay a call on

my old friend Father Duque. I need spiritual guidance. Enjoy yourselves."

Con frowned at Brian's retreating back. "Do you think he's telling the truth?"

"Sure he is. He never really lies, just indulges in many shades of meaning. Eat up; we have to follow him."

"Now, wait a minute. If your old man is going to confession, he doesn't want an entourage."

Deirdre snorted. "He's not going to confession."

"But he said . . ."

" 'Spiritual guidance.' A phrase capable of very wide interpretation. He's up to no good. It's been years since he last saw Father Duque, and you and I know that people change. You're pretty sure he's being blackmailed over something. Priest or no priest, he may be our murderer."

Brian and Dennis were just sitting down comfortably to chat when the rectory doorbell rang.

"Sorry." Dennis got up. "This late in the evening, it may be an emergency." He returned, followed by Con and Deirdre.

"We were just passing by and thought you might like a lift back to Finbar's," Deirdre offered in airy explanation. Con hovered behind her, his face fiery with embarrassment.

"Very thoughtful. Dennis, you've met my daughter but not her husband, Con Connolly."

After courtesies were exchanged and drinks offered and refused, Brian turned to Dennis. "I really do need to have a rather personal chat. Maybe these two could wait in here, if you don't mind. They might spend the time meditating on nosiness."

"You're a fine one to talk," Deirdre interjected. Con just shuffled his feet and looked at the carpet.

Dennis heaved out of his chair to don the purple stole of penance. He touched it to his lips before adjusting it over his shoulders. "We could go to the reconciliation room, or the confessional if you're not one of these newfangled Catholics."

130

"I'm newfangled, no sackcloth and ashes for me. I'm all for contrition in comfort."

Through the closing door, Brian heard Con mutter, "I told you. . . ."

The room off the sacristy was furnished like a comfortable parlor. Dennis sat and raised his hand in blessing.

"Take off your stole and relax. I'm not about to go to confession."

"But you said . . ."

"Personal chat. Not the same thing. Dennis, I've known you since I wet my pants in kindergarten and you covered up by chucking the dirty paint water all over me. I still owe you one for that. You know why I'm here in Fall River. I've poked my nose into a lot of private places and learned a lot of things I'd rather not know."

Dennis's face turned a sickly gray. "What are you getting at?"

"Most of the stuff is none of my business, but I have to sift and evaluate. Hell, not to mince words, I have reason to believe you're being blackmailed . . . and I think I know who the blackmailer is."

"That's impossible."

"What's impossible? That you're being blackmailed or that I know the blackmailer?"

He seemed to shrink in his chair and his voice shook as the mask of a good-natured fat man was stripped away, revealing the raw pain beneath. "I am being blackmailed; it's been going on for years. Not for much longer, thank God."

"What do you mean?"

"You might as well know. I have a cardiac condition. With all this weight, I don't expect to last much longer. Don't feel sorry; it will be a blessing. How did you find out about the blackmail?"

"I can't tell you without betraying someone else and, old friend, I don't have the slightest idea of what this person has on you. I just know that it's going on. Would it help to tell me?"

"You don't understand; I can't tell anyone. The seal of the

confessional is involved." He clapped his hand over his mouth. "Oh my God, I shouldn't even have said that much." He broke down and sobbed.

Brian pulled out his handkerchief and pried the hands away from Dennis's streaming face as he murmured consolation. "Blow," he ordered.

22

BRIAN LAY IN bed in Finbar and André's spare room. He was dead tired. Muscles he'd forgotten he owned were protesting the workout they'd gotten when he went sliding with Verity. He eased himself over on his back and gazed at the ceiling that was fitfully illuminated by the headlights of occasional passing cars. His body ached for sleep, but his racing brain would not let go of Liza's problem. Maire was due home in four days and he had to be at the airport to meet her.

He tried to blank his mind. He counted backward from a thousand. He singsonged mentally through every verse of *The Song of Hiawatha*. He rubbed his stomach clockwise a hundred times. Finally, he gave up the struggle and got up. Past experience had taught him that when all else failed, there was nothing like a brisk walk to soothe the mind and bring sleep.

The small hours are a time apart, he mused as he left the house. As far as he could see, no one was stirring on Globe Street. The mundane workaday scene had become a place of mystery. The dark shadows might hide terrible secrets or unimaginable beauty. Cats padded about on their own affairs. Occasionally a sleeping dog was half-roused at his passage, decided there was no threat, and drooped nose to paws once more. The houses turned blind, bland faces, keeping their secrets well. One direction was as good as another. He turned north.

After a few blocks, he realized he was not alone. The one who followed was not keeping perfect step. The dogs that rose at his passage were grumbling again about thirty seconds later and he realized this had been true ever since he left Globe Street. They/she/he—whoever—must have been watching the house. He glanced back but saw no one. The shadows were very deep. He quickened his pace.

St. Anne's Church was coming into view, taking away the minimal security offered by inhabited houses. When it was pointed out to him by Dennis on his first day in Fall River, he'd been tickled by the magnificent Victorian mishmash of Gothic and Romanesque, pedimented in the Greek manner and topped with twin onion-shaped domes. The place seemed less amusing at two in the morning as it loomed hugely over the street. Directly opposite the church was the entrance to a park.

He raised his eyes to the top of one of the dome-topped towers silhouetted against the glow of the city lights. The massive pile of blue marble seemed to be falling on his head. Then a hand reached from behind him and closed over his wrist.

He jerked back, but the grip on his wrist tightened. A voice whispered, "Cool it, pops, I won't hurt you. I'm old Finbar's cousin and he asked me to keep an eye on you. Let's go for a little 'walkie-talkie' in the park."

Under the streetlight, his captor was revealed as a middle-aged man who had come of age in the sixties and was still firmly stuck in that decade. His graying blond hair was sparse on top and gathered back with a shoelace into a ponytail. His face— what could be seen of it under a bushy blond beard—was weathered to the texture of old leather. Good-humored crinkles framed his twinkling blue eyes. He sported a black nail-studded vest over a T-shirt decorated with a devil's head, as well as black pants that barely made it around his girth. Heavy boots with metal toe caps completed his ensemble. Not the most reassuring type at two in the morning on a lonely street, but Brian felt no menace. And, if he really was Finbar's cousin . . .

134

"A vision no artist could paint. To what, or whom, do I owe the pleasure?" He eased his wrist free and followed across the street.

"Old Finbar was right; you're a real cool cat. I like that. O'Connor's the name, Sean O'Connor. I'm Abby Meyer's cousin, too, from the Irish side of the family."

"And I'm Brian Donodio. I must say you have a dramatic way of making yourself known."

"Sorry about that. Finbar asked me to keep an eye on things, like quietly, you know."

"He didn't say anything to me about you."

"He didn't want you to know. He thought you might, like, resent it."

"And he might have been right. I knew someone was following me and I'm glad it turned out to be you. I was getting a little worried."

Sean grabbed his arm again and pulled him along. "Let's get back here on the grass out of the light," he whispered. "All I was doing was watching the house. I saw you come out, then I spotted this other dude who fell right in behind you. That's when I decided to see what was coming down and tagged along. The dude stopped at a bush to take a leak. That's when I zipped ahead on the other side so I could catch up and pull you off the street." Sean stood and peered over at the church. "He's camped out now in front of St. Anne's. Looks like a cop to me."

"Why on earth would a cop be following me? Anyway, how can you tell he's a cop?"

"Takes one to know one."

"You mean you're . . ."

"MP in Nam. I've gone straight ever since, but some things stay with a man. Here comes a car to pick him up; he must have called in that he lost you."

Brian watched. Sure enough, a squad car glided in toward the curb and the man stepped in.

"He'll lose brownie points on this one. Where are you going, anyway?"

"Nowhere, just walking. I couldn't sleep."

"Just walking isn't very bright in this town. Why don't we

go to my place and talk? I get antsy in the park at this hour."

"Why not, indeed. Where is your place?"

"Don't expect anything grand. It's down by Cook Pond."

"Cook Pond?"

"South of Globe Street. It's where they hide the bodies."

They retraced their route to Globe Street where Sean had left his motorcycle, a vintage Harley-Davidson. "Have you ever ridden on one of these?"

Brian eyed it doubtfully. "Can't say that I have."

"Nothing to it, man. Sorry, I only have one helmet. If I'd known I was taking you for a ride, I'd have brought my old lady's."

"Your old lady?"

"Yeah, her name's Phoebe, but I call her Babe." He swung his leg over the machine and kicked back the stand. "Hop aboard, man. Hook your hands in my belt. I'll take it slow and easy."

"How will, er, your good lady feel about having her home invaded at this hour?" The motor kicked to life and Sean's reply was lost in the *vroom.*

They roared along Plymouth Avenue, then turned into a secondary street. Brian's fingers tightened in a death grip on Sean's belt. If this was slow and easy, what was fast and furious? Small cottages alternated with three-decker tenements. Industrial dinosaurs of closed textile mills loomed up and fell behind, mute testimony to former industrial greatness. Finally, they slowed to trace their way through a narrow alley between two tenements.

Dark clouds had blown up to obscure the faint starlight. Brian sensed the freedom of open space, but even with his night vision, he could see no more than vague outlines. He closed his eyes and breathed deeply.

The overlying impression was water, not stagnant, but definitely polluted—thick with algae. An oak tree contributed its distinctive acidic tang. He detected freshly turned earth and a vague chemical taint. Gasoline or oil? Must be from one of the industrial sites they'd passed. A sharp, musky reek: Either a skunk had passed by lately or this was a favorite hangout of lovesick tom cats. He could form no clear picture.

"Wait here a minute while I turn on the lights. I don't want you tripping over something."

He did as he was told, not knowing what to expect but vastly intrigued. Vague associations with the word *pad* flitted through his head. Maybe a shanty? A 1930s run-down bungalow? A messy back apartment house? An electric glow suddenly plucked at his closed lids.

A rustic fence enclosed a log cabin approached by a brick walk. On one side was the oak tree he had smelled, a real lalapalooza over seventy feet tall. How had it escaped when its siblings crashed down to serve as raw material for ships and houses? Alongside the fence and on each side of the path were the beds of a perennial border, already cut back and mulched with compost and hay.

"Your eyes are dropping out of your head, man." Sean came down the path, grinning from ear to ear.

"Well you must admit it's eye-popping. I don't know what I expected, but it certainly wasn't this."

"Built it myself." His face had a modest "it's really nothing" expression. "Come on in."

"What about Mrs. O'Connor? This is a very strange hour to come calling."

"No sweat. Babe's away visiting her folks in California and she took the kids. I'm just an old bachelor right now."

The front door opened directly into a living room dominated by a stone fireplace. Navajo rugs glowed against the gleaming honey-colored floors. Dangling from the high beamed ceiling was a Calder mobile with his signature red and black shapes.

Brian pointed. He sounded almost accusatory. "That's a Calder."

"Yeah. Sandy gave it to us as a wedding present. I did some casting for him before I went to Nam."

"You're an artist?"

"Sculptor. I teach at the Rhode Island School of Design."

137

His belly jiggled up and down with mirth. "Did you think I was some kind of yahoo?"

That was precisely what Brian had thought, but he'd rather die than admit it. "Of course not."

"You did, too. Cop a squat, man. Let's talk."

"You say you're Abby Meyer's cousin."

"Yeah, man. Her mom and mine were sisters."

"Were you close?"

"Abby was a lot younger, a kid. And then, she was different."

"Different?"

"She was brought up Jewish. It was like a cultural difference, you know what I mean? But I was real fond of her."

"Which brings me to the important question. Why would someone want to kill her? Everyone I've spoken to liked her. She was doing well in her real estate business. Why? There's no way Liza Borden could have done it. I've known her since she was a teenager."

"Every murderer has people who've known them forever."

"Aside from the fact that it just isn't in Liza to do something like that, she's too smart. She'd never be caught red-handed."

Sean started to interrupt. "No, hear me out. Who called the cops? No one seems to know. If Liza is the murderer, would she have axed Abby, gone to a phone to call the cops, and returned to stand over the body with the murder weapon in her hand? I'm sorry, it just won't wash. So, tell me about the O'Connor family."

"You look beat, man. How about I make us some coffee? It's a long story."

"I have to be at work in a few hours. Let's get on with it."

"Coffee first." Sean set out mugs and poured coffee into the machine. When they were settled with steaming mugs, he took a deep gulp and started his tale. "Like I said, it's a long story. Margie O'Connor, my grandmother, had four children. Mary, who was Abby's mother. Agnes, who was my mother, and twin boys, Liam and Patrick. They were older."

"Liam and Patrick?"

Sean shifted uneasily. "I can't tell you too much about

138

them. There was something funny there; Aunt Mary and Ma never mentioned them. I got the idea they were adopted by a family—or families—who moved away from Fall River and may have changed their names. I do know that Ma always changed the subject when I asked any questions about them."

"If you'll pardon my saying so, you seem uncomfortable talking about your family."

"There's a saying, Old sins have long shadows. Hell, it's all in the past now, but the O'Connors, my branch of them anyway, were dirt here in Fall River. Do you know anything about Bedford Street?"

"Tell me."

"That's where the O'Connors lived. Marge O'Connor, my grandmother, was never married—neither was my mother. That's why my name is still O'Connor. Aunt Mary, the one who married Bernard Meyer, was different. She got out, finished high school, and got a respectable job.

"For years, she wouldn't have anything to do with us and my folks cut her dead. See, she converted to Judaism when she married Meyer, and you know how Catholics felt about that back then, even if they didn't go to church themselves." His face reddened at the memory. "Then, when she was expecting Abby, she made up with her mother and sister. Ma died about five years ago."

"But what has this to do with Abby's murder?"

"It's the only connection I can come up with. See, Grandma Marge wasn't like my mother. She was what they called a 'kept woman.' "

"Who kept her?"

"Who else? Jack Delaney. I'll say this for the old boy: He left her well fixed."

The gears inside Brian's head shifted. Pieces of the puzzle dropped into place. He didn't have the whole answer, and he had not one shred of evidence, but he had a darn good idea. "This means that you're Delaney's grandson?"

"Not that I'm proud of it."

Brian was no longer tired. His adrenaline was flowing, but

139

he had to get away and think. "It's been an enlightening chat. I think I'll mosey back to Globe Street."

"I'll run you back on the Harley."

"No need. I'll be perfectly all right."

"Sure you don't want a lift? It's no trouble."

"I'm sure. But I'm worried about your safety now. Lock up tight and watch your back."

Sean roared with laughter. "Who would want to hurt me?"

Going through the alley, Brian sensed movement. He paused, irresolute, and nearly turned back. He strained his eyes into the shadows but saw nothing, shrugged, and continued on.

There was no point going to bed. A long hot shower and a change into his Delaney uniform somewhat restored him, though he knew he would crash later. He wouldn't have slept, anyway. His brain was racing and he could hear what sounded like dozens of fire engines whooping south along Plymouth Avenue. He decided to get the coffee on for André and Finbar.

He snapped on the radio in the kitchen to catch the news and was listening with half an ear to the latest self-serving explanations from Washington when a local voice interrupted the accentless newspeak of the network commentator.

"We interrupt this program for a local bulletin. Firefighters responding to an alarm after five this morning were unable to save the residence of Sean O'Connor.

"Mr. O'Connor is a well-known local sculptor and teacher at the Rhode Island School of Design. He lived in a log house fronting Cook Pond and he is the owner of two large tenements on the property. One of his tenants, Mrs. Jeanne Lemieux, stated that she was awakened by the smell of smoke and called in the alarm. She also stated that Mrs. Phoebe O'Connor and the couple's two children are in California visiting Mrs. O'Connor's parents.

"Firefighters at the scene have not yet been able to enter the remains of the house to see if anybody was inside at the

140

time of the fire. The arson squad is withholding judgment, but a spokesman stated that the preliminary investigation disclosed signs of a suspicious fire. Stay tuned and we will keep you up to date on further developments. We now return you to the network broadcast in progress. . . ."

Brian crossed himself. He had no doubt that Sean was dead. Two of Delaney's grandchildren gone. What about Liam and Patrick O'Connor, the boys who were adopted? Had they left children? Or were they still very much alive? Did they know who they were? Were they both adopted by the same family? Adoption records were often sealed by the court, particularly when someone involved was locally important.

He broke eggs into a bowl for scrambling. You can't make an omelette without breaking eggs. Well, someone was sure making an omelette here in Fall River. The coffeemaker pinged. Still deep in thought, he turned it off automatically. Abby Meyer's death had aroused little emotion. He hadn't known her. To him, she was just the occasion of framing Liza. But, by hell, he'd met Sean and liked him. He had two small children who called him Father. He had a wife who would never be the same from this day on.

He'd been amused at the man's hippie affectations and at his grammar that slipped into standard English when he forgot he was a big bad biker. The man was an artist and a fellow teacher. The more he thought about it, the angrier he got.

It was almost light outside. Finbar and André would be up soon. Maybe he should call Finbar. After all, Sean was his cousin. No, let him sleep. Sean might have escaped, and there was no point getting the man all upset prematurely. His attention sharpened. They were interrupting again.

". . . an update on the fire at Cook Pond. The body of a man has been recovered from the waters of Cook Pond, but police are withholding his identity pending the notification of his next of kin. Preliminary examination of the body suggests that the cause of death was cardiac arrest, not the superficial burns on the body. Here with me now is Captain William McGuire, the head of the Major Crime Unit of the Fall River Police Department. Captain McGuire . . ."

141

"In the wake of this tragic fire, I am asking anyone who knows how to contact Mrs. Phoebe O'Connor to get in touch with my office. I wish to emphasize that we are not yet sure that a crime has been committed. This intelligence has to wait on the report of the arson investigators and the medical examiner. As of now, it is officially classified as an accident . . . a tragic accident."

"Tragic accident, my aunt Fanny!" Brian muttered. He heard footsteps approaching the kitchen.

"Is that coffee I smell?" Finbar scooted in like a skinny gray badger. "You're up early."

"I've never been to bed. Sit down and let me get you some coffee and eggs."

"Such service. I'd like to keep you here."

"You may change your mind." He poured himself a mug and sat down on the other side of the table. "I couldn't sleep last night, so I went for a walk. Someone, a cop, I think, followed me. So did Sean O'Connor. He told me you asked him to keep an eye on things, and on me particularly."

"So?"

"I think he's dead."

All the color drained from Finbar's face. He put his mug carefully on the table. "What did you say?"

"There's no gentle way to break bad news. I'm very sorry, but it's true. I went back with him to Cook Pond so we could talk. He offered to run me back here on his Harley, but I refused. I wish to God I hadn't."

"How did he die? He was all right when you left?"

"Of course he was. I heard it over the radio while I was making breakfast. There was a fire after I left and it may have been arson. They just announced that a man's body was recovered from the water and the police are withholding identification pending notification of the next of kin."

"I have to get over there."

"Bill McGuire was on the radio just now asking anyone who knows where Phoebe is to get in touch. Do you know?"

"Yes." He pushed away from the table.

"I'll change out of my Delaney uniform and come with you."

142

23

CON AND DEIRDRE were to meet them at Cook Pond. By daylight, the place was stripped of the hints of mystery and charm Brian had perceived in the small hours. The murky water seemed made for murder. Anything hidden there would be lost for the ages.

It was a good-sized pond, irregularly oval in shape and home to the premises of several heavy construction companies. A spanking-new school and an armory overlooked the north end. Several old mill buildings, now converted to other uses, showed that the water had provided power to many looms during the palmy days of textile greatness. The few cottages had yards so choked with heavy bushes that they were completely hidden from the pond's edge.

Rubbery plantain grass, the tough ruderal growth that arrived in the New World as a stowaway in the luggage of European settlers, yielded under Brian and Finbar's feet, to rise unbroken when pressure was released. Plumed phragmites clustered thickly at the water's verge, strong opportunists that thrived in less-than-ideal conditions. A turtle's head broke the surface.

The exception to this disorder had been Sean's log cabin. His land was cleared and showed evidence of devoted care, now marred by the depredations of fire equipment and heavy boots. Brian was glad to see that the noble oak had escaped with only minimal scorching along one side. Of the house itself, nothing was left but a pile of still-smoking timber and the stone chimney.

Deirdre hailed him. "Dad, what have you been up to now?" Con made a shushing motion.

"And a good morning to you, daughter. Is that any way to speak to your old father, who's been up all night?"

"Why were you up all night?"

"I was being entertained until after three by the late Sean O'Connor in this house that burned down shortly after I left."

"You'll have to tell whoever's in charge of the investigation," Con interrupted.

"That poses a problem. I'm due at Delaney in thirty-five minutes to start my day's work. Bill McGuire is here, and if it turns out, as I'm sure it will, that Sean was murdered, he'll be in charge. I don't wish to speak with him because I don't think he realizes that Brian MacMorrough, the slightly disreputable jobbing gardener, is also Dr. Brian Donodio, the representative on TV of the Borden family."

Con growled, "Don't be too sure of that."

"I'm not, particularly after last night. However, he hasn't challenged me and I want to keep it that way." He made a gesture at his suit, tie, and white shirt. "I chucked my work clothes into the back of the car. I hadn't grown the beard when I was on TV, but a cop is trained to look beyond such things."

"Why don't I speak with him?" Finbar suggested. "I have to give him Phoebe's address in California and he might give me some idea of what's going on. After all, they haven't decided officially that a crime has been committed."

Deirdre added, "You can speak with the arson people, Dad. Tell them what you know. That way you're covered, then you can leave for work ASAP. I'll wait for you here. I don't want to be seen talking to you guys, because McGuire's met me already and he thinks I'm a freelance writer."

Brian had a last word with Finbar. "I think you should call

144

Phoebe yourself and advise her to leave the children with their grandparents for a while."

"Why?"

"She's not in danger, but they are. I'm quite sure that if those kids came back here before this business is cleared up, they'll be the next to have a nasty accident."

He pulled Con aside. "You're sure you understand the story we cooked up on the phone?"

"I still don't like it."

"What's not to like? There are two small children in California who'll be next if we don't do something."

As soon as Brian joined the fire investigators, he knew it was arson. He could smell kerosene like a sickly underlay to the odors of charred wood, burned fabric, and melted metal. If only he had followed his nose earlier in the day when he thought he smelled oil or gasoline, Sean might still be alive. What he had smelled was probably the stored flammable ready for use. Had it been already sloshed round the house when they entered, there'd be no way he could have missed it.

Three men clad in civilian clothes but wearing the distinctive heavy boots of firefighters were clustered round the soaked, charred mess that had been a porch. One of them, obviously the senior man in charge, was pointing with his pen at a rough plan drawn on graph paper. "See that?" The pen followed a twisting line around the floor plan of the house. "What the char lines show and given the speed with which the house was totaled, I figure he sloshed the gas all around the foundation on the outside and finished up with lobbing an incendiary device through the window. Right there." The pen stabbed impatiently.

Brian coughed. "Er . . . excuse me."

The man looked up. "Yes, may I help you?" He grinned. "I know you're not the guy from Beacon Mutual, not dressed like that."

"No. My name's Donodio, Brian Donodio."

145

"And mine's Theodore Monck." The smile stayed in place, but there was a testy edge to his voice. "As you can see, we're busy." He rolled his shoulders under his plaid flannel shirt in a tension-releasing gesture.

"I just thought I should mention that I was here with Mr. O'Connor, God rest his soul, until shortly after three this morning."

"You don't say. Well, let's go off to the side here where we can have a quiet word." He turned to his associates. "You guys keep on with what we were doing."

Brian looked sadly down at the twisted, distorted shapes of the Calder mobile that had been recovered and bagged in plastic, mute testimony to the searing heat of the flames. "The last time I saw that, it was hanging in Sean's living room."

"Well, it's evidence now. What was it?"

"A Calder mobile."

"Valuable?"

"Very. And Sean was very proud of it."

They sat down at a picnic table near the edge of the water. "Now, suppose you tell me about last night."

Brian told the truth with certain omissions, ending with a small cat to put among the pigeons: ". . . and, one last thing, did you know that Sean was a cousin of Abby Meyer?"

"So?"

"Well, it gives one food for thought."

"Maybe you'd better have a word with Bill McGuire."

"I probably should, but there's somewhere I have to be and he'll be busy for hours. You have my name and know how to get in touch." He got up and made his way to the car, expecting any moment to be summoned back.

Deirdre was waiting by his car. "Drive me over to Delaney while I change in the back. Then you can take the car back to Finbar's and let Con meet you there." There were muffled grunts and thumps as he wriggled into his uniform and ratty sneakers.

"I have another favor for you to ask José. Tell him we need

146

to know about any trust funds established by Jack Delaney for two boys, who administers them, the amount, and how the money is paid. The birth names of the boys are Liam and Patrick O'Connor. I understand they were adopted years ago and I don't know their adoptive names."

"Both by the same family?"

"I don't know that, either. He may have to go as far back as the 1920s. Tell him to try the local banks first or State Street in Boston. He may find nothing, so I'm going another route."

"How about adoption records?"

"I doubt if stuff that far back would be in the data banks. The records are probably getting moldy in some basement, but he can try."

"He's going to be sorry he ever offered."

"No, he won't. He and Rosa are sitting on a gold mine with those tapestries Rosa makes. Wait until I tell your mother about them and she zips up here to talk turkey. He'll fall in love with us all over again."

"You sound positively mercenary."

"And what's wrong with that? I just hate to see such a talent not being used. Let me off here. I'll walk the rest of the way."

Bevilaqua was deep in the compilation of his quarterly report. Steve Springer was pruning trees. Brian was supposed to be mulching the flower beds for their long winter's nap. Instead, he was swigging coffee with Joshua and Ira. He hadn't wanted to be seen going into the gatehouse, so the three of them were hanging out in a storage shed.

He brought them up to date on the intelligence gleaned during his busy Sunday. "You two, Phil Dobbs, and Dennis Duque are the only ones I can really trust and, I must admit, I have a slight doubt about Dennis. I'm almost positive that I know who the murderer is. What I need now is proof."

The two men hanging on his words reacted differently. Joshua turned so pale that Brian was afraid he'd pass out.

"Get your head down. Ira! Take care of him!"

147

Ira ducked Joshua's head between his knees with an ungentle shove. "I knew you'd do it. Who is the bastard?"

Brian ignored the question. "I need proof. I'm pretty sure I have motive, opportunity and means are easy, but I don't have a scintilla of proof."

"We'll get proof."

"But how? Ira, are you game for another spot of skulduggery?"

24

BRIAN STRAIGHTENED HIS aching back and gazed at the neatly dug flower beds. It was time to quit this job. The core of the investigation had moved away from the Delaney Institute. He had gone without rest for at least thirty-three hours and he was too old for this type of punishment.

Bevilaqua was still poring over his report. Brian coughed.

"Yes? Can't you see I'm busy and can't talk to you now. Get back to work."

Wunderbar. The man's rudeness took away Brian's guilt at leaving him shorthanded. "I quit."

"You can't do that."

"Sure I can." He too off his badge and laid it on the desk with his locker key. "Here. I already cleared my locker. I'll give the uniform to Finbar." It felt good to walk out the door and leave Bevilaqua openmouthed.

First things first. He picked up his clothes and car at Finbar's and returned to the Holiday Inn just in time to bid Con farewell. "I wish you could stick around, and I'm sure Deirdre wishes it even more heartily. With any luck, we'll be done here in a couple of days. How did your session with the cops go?"

"Just as you expected. They thought I was some kind of a nut. And I felt like one, telling them I was Sean's cousin without a sliver of proof."

"Nonsense. What sort of proof of cousinhood do people usually carry around with them? At least the story put another layer of protection around Sean's kids, if we're right and someone is really intent on rubbing out all Jack Delaney's direct descendants."

Con grinned. " 'Rubbing out,' I like that. Your language is getting very colorful but, if I may say so, a little dated. The expression of choice these days is *wasted.*"

"Well, I've quit my job at Delaney's. Now I'm going to crash for a few hours. I don't think I've been this tired since the Battle of the Bulge."

He slept dreamlessly until six o'clock Tuesday morning, awakening with a ravenous appetite and a sense of time running out. Maire was due at La Guardia Airport on Thursday evening and he had promised to meet her. He needed an ally with clout. He needed proof. He needed a large breakfast to fortify him for the day ahead. He picked up the phone and asked to be connected first with Deirdre, then with Dobbs. Finally, he showered and shaved off his beard. Halfway through, he regretted it; he should have saved the beard for Maire.

Over coffee, orange juice, home fries, and scrambled eggs, he gave them their marching orders.

"First, I want to lay out the case for you the way I see it. Make a list. If you two have anything to add, now is the time." He whipped his trusty yellow pad out of his briefcase.

"One: Our objective is to prove that Liza Borden did not murder Abby Meyer. In order to do this, we have to prove that the murders of Abby and Sean O'Connor are connected. That connection would be ipso facto proof of Liza's innocence. So far—we hope—our activities have managed to escape the notice of the murderer.

"Two: Liza was framed for Abby's murder because, as Abby's best friend, investigation might reveal a motive and, maybe, because the murderer has a warped sense of humor and could not resist the coincidence of her name and the Fall

River milieu. Most importantly, framing Liza strikes another blow at Delaney's already precarious financial situation.

"Three: The Delaney Institute was targeted in order to force its closing under the terms of Mrs. Delaney's will if it failed in its purpose of research into and preservation of endangered species. The stealing of the bears by Leander Seward caused donations to the institute to fall off. This inspired our killer to mutilate and kill other animals so donations would further decline and Delaney's name would become a hissing and a byword to other institutions. The police position is that the murder and the dead animals are two totally unrelated crimes. I think the framing of Liza was a master touch of adverse publicity. If the institute closes, the money reverts to the next of kin. Caspar Lovelace told me that the net worth of the estate is around fifty million.

"Four: Who are the beneficiaries if this should happen? The Delaney family is enormous, with hundreds of known members. Those we know who are directly concerned with the institute are Finbar O'Hanlon, who has a dream of buying Bowhead College, and who, though he has a very comfortable income, is extended financially to the breaking point. Caspar Lovelace himself told me that Mrs. Delaney was his aunt, though he also pointed out that he is out of the running, as he is related on the distaff side and not a Delaney by blood. I think we can rule him out. Abby Meyer, God rest her, was old Jack Delaney's granddaughter on the wrong side of the blanket. Her grandmother was Marge O'Connor, who was Delaney's mistress. Killing Abby got one direct descendant out of the way.

"Five: Let's take a look at Marge O'Connor. What I know so far is that she bore four children to Delaney. Two daughters, Mary and Agnes, and twin boys, Liam and Patrick. The boys were the eldest and were given up for adoption. Mary got out of the Bedford Street trap, improved her lot in life, and married Bernard Meyer. Agnes never married. Sean was discreet, but I gathered that his mother was a lady of the evening. With his death yesterday, two heirs were out of the way.

"This is why it's imperative that Sean's children stay in

151

California, where they're safe. The two boys, Liam and Patrick, are the wild cards. Sean told me that they were adopted by a family, or families, who may have changed their names and probably moved out of Fall River. If they're still alive they would be men in their sixties, probably with children and grandchildren of their own. That's why I had Con tell the police he was Sean's cousin; it can't hurt to float the rumor of another descendant. Has either of you anything to add?"

Dobbs clapped, causing heads to turn. Their waitress came running over. "Did you need anything, sir?"

"I'm terribly sorry. I would certainly never be so rude as to clap to get your attention. I was applauding my friend here." The waitress shook her head and moved away. "That was a masterly exposition, but I still don't know whodunit. I do think, though, that Finbar's out of the running."

"I admit that I don't think he's a very likely murderer, but why do you think he's out of the running?"

"This is in confidence. He has a sister who's in an institution here in town. It's a sad story. She's a lot younger. When he was a young man and she was just a toddler, she ran out into the driveway just as he was backing out. It wasn't his fault, but he felt responsible. When his parents died, she could no longer be cared for at home and the price of private care has gone up much faster than his income."

"At the risk of sounding heartless," Deirdre interposed, "that just underlines his need for money."

"She's right, you know. And there's his scheme to take over Bowhead."

"Gardeners aren't murderers," Dobbs averred.

"I had a run-in with a magnificent gardener in Ireland who was a miserable criminal and an accessory to murder, so the two things aren't mutually exclusive. But I agree that he's a long shot."

Dobbs shook his head. "You know the academic grapevine. I heard a rumor that he'll replace Seward as president of Bowhead and the trustees will confirm his selection at their next meeting. He'll be in line for a much larger salary and he'll get control of the college without having to bid for it."

152

"He had no way of knowing that all this would happen at the time of Abby's murder."

Dobbs opened his mouth to argue, but Deirdre cut him off. "I follow your scenario, Dad. What's your game plan?"

A pained look blossomed on Brian's face. "Do you have to use those dreadful Reaganisms? This is not a game, nor is it a screenplay. Do you have any more material from José?"

"I do indeed," she answered smugly as she flourished a sheaf of computer printouts. "You were right on the money—two trust funds paid right out of a local bank for over sixty years. And they're substantial." She ran a gleeful finger over the entries. "See—names, addresses, the whole megillah."

Brian pored over the sheets. "Do you see what this means? Now we have two candidates for murderer."

"Maybe not," Dobbs offered, "it might be a conspiracy."

25

Brian was on his way back to Boston. He had an eleven o'clock appointment with Caspar Lovelace at his office on State Street. At one o'clock, he was to lunch with Abby's aunt, Susan Meyer.

A discreet bronze plaque announced the presence of Lovelace, Cabot and Kerrigan, Attorneys at Law. The walnut-paneled elevator had a padded bench for passengers and was ensconced in a glassed-in shaft framed in wrought iron. It was operated by an ancient lady in a black dress with a white collar. She closed the inside gate and turned the handle. Brian felt the ambience deserved the old-fashioned courtesy of hat removal. He stood with his fedora over his heart and watched the bronze arrow on the semicircular dial inch up to the fifth floor.

Caspar Lovelace met him at the door. "Donodio, my dear fellow, I dropped everything when you called. I'm all ears. Come this way."

He led him past a reception desk presided over by a Boston lady of uncertain years. She spared Brian one raking glance through glasses attached to her nonexistent bosom by a silver chain. "Mr. Lovelace."

"Yes, Mrs. Quimp."

"There are several calls."

"Later. Please hold all my calls for the next hour, and if you could manage some coffee for Dr. Donodio and me, I would be most grateful."

"Certainly, Mr. Lovelace. Do you take cream and sugar, Dr. Donodio?"

"Black will be fine."

"Wonderful woman," he said as he led Brian into his office. "Keeps me up to the mark."

The office was straight out of the mid-nineteenth century. Paneled walls framed a cozy fireplace surmounted by a portrait in oils of a peruked worthy sporting white knee breeches, buff coat, and a ruffled lace jabot. Lovelace gestured to the picture.

"My something-great-grandfather, the first Caspar Lovelace and the founder of the firm. He was in the first class to graduate from Harvard College. Of course"—he looked around deprecatingly—"you realize these are not the original offices. There was a fire and we've been here only since 1850." He sat behind a huge partners desk. "Sit down and be comfortable. What may I do for you?"

Brian detailed what had passed since he had visited the Acorn Street house. "So I'm asking if you would reconsider opening Mrs. Delaney's letter. Normally, I would never ask such a thing, but these are exceptional circumstances. There have already been two murders and the lives of Sean O'Connor's two little children may be in danger."

"It would be betraying my professional trust."

"I never had the honor of knowing Mrs. Delaney, but you did. From your knowledge of her, would she have wanted her instructions obeyed to the letter if it might mean the lives of two children?"

"You drive a hard bargain."

"I'm a hard man. Tell you what. I don't want to read her letter myself. You read it and tell me if these names"—he passed a slip of paper over the desk—"are in it. If they're not, I'll forget we ever had this conversation."

Lovelace groaned. "You win." He pressed the intercom.

155

"Mrs. Quimp, when you bring the coffee would you mind also bringing the sealed envelope from the Delaney file?"

"The sealed envelope, Mr. Lovelace?" Disapproval and affront surged through the wire.

"Yes, Mrs. Quimp, the sealed envelope."

Brian had an hour to kill before he met Representative Susan Meyer at La Mangeoire Restaurant on Charles Street. He strolled through the Public Gardens down to the lagoon, only to discover that the swan boats had packed it in for the season.

Balked of this diversion, he turned his attention to the State House standing in golden-domed splendor atop Beacon Hill. Why not? He hadn't been there in years. He set off briskly across the Common.

What would old Bullfinch think if he could see Boston today, he mused. Would he be sad or impressed? He paid tribute to the Sacred Cod enshrined in the House of Representatives. The wooden effigy, symbol of the maritime wealth of the Commonwealth, was older than the chamber in which it hung. If he remembered correctly, the State House dated to 1799 but the codfish went back to 1784, the year Congress ratified the peace treaty between England and the infant American republic.

He glanced at his watch—only fifteen minutes until he was to meet with Representative Meyer. He galloped down the wide staircase with its elegant black iron railings, out into the sunshine, and beat Ms. Meyer to the restaurant with about thirty seconds to spare.

"Abby was a darling girl, Dr. Donodio. The whole family is devastated, not only by her death but the manner of it. And none of us believes for a minute that Liza Borden had anything to do with it."

He surveyed his lunch partner. She was a neat, small woman in late middle age. Her gray hair was drawn back from her face in a tidy bun. Her brown eyes seemed made for

156

humor; he could see the laugh lines at their edges and around her wide mouth, but now they were shadowed with pain. She wore a dark green suit paired with a rusty-colored silk blouse. Her only jewelry was a wide wedding ring.

"I've known Liza since she was a spotty-faced adolescent with an uncorrected overbite. I know the whole family, and I cannot believe she's guilty, either."

"I don't want to hurry you, but I have a committee meeting at two-thirty." She picked up the menu. "Let's order and then we can talk. I can recommend the grinders. I think I'll have pepper-and-egg and an iced cappuccino."

Brian beckoned to the hovering waitress.

"Now, let's get down to business. How may I help you?"

He filled her in on his discoveries to date. "So what I need is someone with clout—someone who has the ear of the higher authorities in Fall River, or Bristol County, or the Commonwealth of Massachusetts."

"I hear you. Let's finish and go back to my office. The attorney general owes me one."

"You're sure it's not an imposition?"

"Quite sure. That bastard in Fall River has been a thorn in my side for a long time. I'll have to do some fast talking to convince the attorney general, but it will be a pleasure."

Back to Fall River to muster the troops. Ira, Dennis, Dobbs, and Deirdre gathered at the Holiday Inn. Finbar had classes; André had work. A quiet word to Rebecca shunted Joshua into a conference.

"Ira, your name should be David; then we'd have an alliterative army and could call this D day. I'm nattering; forgive me. Our pigeon, if he is our pigeon, has a summer house in Rhode Island. The invaluable José found out that he pays property taxes to the town of Bristol. So if we want everything—"

Dobbs finished the sentence: "Shipshape and Bristol fashion?"

"You took the words out of my mouth."

"Predictable. Finish your thought."

"I suggest that the five of us take a little trip. My bet is that he would keep anything incriminating there instead of at his place in Fall River, where it might be found."

Ira was gung ho. The objections came from Dennis and Deirdre.

"It's awfully risky, Dad. And he may keep his stuff in a safe-deposit box."

"What if we're caught? Our new bishop is a great guy, but I think he would be very unhappy if one of his priests was caught breaking and entering."

"And so he should be. Let's not get caught."

"What's your plan? And shouldn't we let Joshua in on this?" Ira was fidgeting back and forth in his chair.

"No disrespect to your brother-in-law, but I think he has too nervous a temperament for this undertaking. Rebecca is keeping him occupied. I think we should all pile into Ira's wagon and case the joint. My hope is that the place will be reasonably isolated. Then, with luck and in the absence of nosy neighbors, Deirdre, Dennis, and I will return after dark in Dennis's beat-up old parish work van."

"Good point, Dad. Anyone who's seen the wagon earlier in the day won't connect it with a van at night."

Dennis warmed to the planning. "I'll smear the license plates with mud."

"And I have a tiny camera I use for bird photography and some infrared film," Ira added.

"No. You and Dobbs will not be coming with us."

Dobbs reared up like an enraged turkey cock. "Just a minute—"

Ira interrupted. "She's *my* sister. . . ."

"Gently, gently. I want you and Dobbs to follow us in case we're interrupted. We need an ace in the hole."

"I'll take my gun," Deirdre offered.

Four shocked faces turned on her; four voices spoke as one: "No gun."

"What do you mean? I always carry my gun."

"You know you're not licensed now you've left the INS. Does Con know you're still carrying?"

158

Deirdre made a face. "Don't *you* get on my case. I feel naked without it."

"Well, you'll just have to put up with a little indecent exposure. I don't want any complications from the Rhode Island cops. I have authority only here in the Bay State."

"What authority?" Deirdre demanded.

This was his moment. "To quote the advice you and Con were always giving me over that little affair I was mixed up in last summer, 'Leave it to the professionals.' I am now a special investigator for the Commonwealth of Massachusetts and if you're a good girl, I might deputize you."

The afternoon's reconnaissance was highly satisfactory. Ground zero was an isolated cottage overlooking Mount Hope Bay. Seven o'clock found the three returning there in Dennis's artistically muddied van, with Dobbs and Ira following. In the event they were stopped and questioned, they had agreed on a story: They were birders who had been told of a sighting on the coast near Bristol of a horned grebe, a species on the Audubon Society's Blue List. They were hoping to sneak up on the bird because none of them had it on their lifetime lists. If they were stopped by an officer who happened to be a birder, then they'd have to wing it.

No one stopped them. It was just as well, the rain that had been forecast all day started to fall steadily. Their story would not have held water. Dennis doused the headlights and drove slowly down the muddy track to where the cottage loomed, dark and shuttered, at the water's edge.

"Dennis, we'll follow the same routine we did with the bears. Park the van out of sight and we'll check in with you every fifteen minutes on the walkie-talkie."

They waited in the shadow of the encroaching bushes until their night sight sharpened. Their hooded dark sweatshirts and jeans were darkened still further by the rain until they were indistinguishable from the shade around them. They were so still that the night creatures that had withdrawn at their approach took heart and started to go about their business. The dripping undergrowth was filled with soft rustlings and cries.

"Dad," Deirdre whispered, "let's get on with it. I'm getting antsy."

"Why does it always have to rain when we pull these capers?" He gestured her forward. "Try to find an unfastened shutter. I wish we'd been able to bring André along; we could use his talent with locks."

"I'm no slouch in that department myself." Deirdre made a dash for the padlocked front door.

"What are you doing?"

"Hold the light for me," she answered impatiently. "Shine it down and shield it while I get to work." She pulled a ring of picklocks out of her pocket. "A lock gun would be handier, but I don't have one. I sneaked these out of Con's stuff before I left New York. It never hurts to be prepared." She probed carefully. "This is an expensive padlock; usually they can be opened with a bobby pin à la Nancy Drew. Ah, gotcha." There was a faint click as the wards yielded.

The interior was pitch-black and cold with the dry, musty smell of a closed house. The flashlight revealed shabby furniture swathed in plastic. A lean-to kitchen opened off the central room and another door led to a bathroom with a claw-footed tub and necessarium surmounted by a high wooden tank.

Brian closed the door carefully and pulled the string hanging from the unshaded central fixture, to no avail.

"Utilities are off. I hope that means we won't be disturbed. Quickly and quietly now. We're looking for any papers relating to adoption as long ago as sixty years or more, and anything to do with the Delaney estate or institute."

The kitchen cabinets held nothing but clean dishes, canned goods, and a few half-full boxes of cereal. In the main room, plastic-covered mattresses and cushions were piled in a neat heap and a metal plate protected the fireplace from the intrusions of birds and squirrels. The drawers in a couple of chests were innocent of anything remotely suspicious.

Brian was not happy. "It looks like we've drawn a blank. Let's go."

"Wait," Deirdre called from the bathroom. "I think I may have something."

The radio on Brian's belt crackled and came to life. "Come in, Brian. Over." Dennis's voice sounded strained.

"Brian here. What's up?"

"There's a car coming down the track."

"Deirdre, leave whatever you're doing and come. We have to get out of here."

It was the work of a minute to close the door and snap the padlock in place. Outside, the rain still fell and thunder grumbled in the distance. They sloshed up the side of the muddy track, ready at any moment to slip into the bushes on the side. Why couldn't they hear the approaching car? A flash of lightning showed them the van sheltered under an overhanging tree and they broke into a run.

Just as they reached the van, a man stepped from its shadow and the headlights flashed on. His face was distorted and disguised by a stocking mask. "Okay, Donodio, MacMorrough, or whatever the hell your name is, don't try anything funny. You and the girl get into the van. We need to have a little talk." He made an impatient gesture with his gun.

Brian took a deep breath through his nose. Now he was certain. He only hoped that he lived to see his theory vindicated.

161

26

"I'M SORRY. THEY pulled a gun on me and made me call and tell you a car was coming." Dennis gulped out his excuse as he was shoved roughly into the back of the van by a second masked man.

"Shut up, you." The man reinforced his command with a stinging slap across the priest's ample buttocks, which sent him sprawling across the metal floor.

"Would it be out of order to ask where we're going?" Brian was not about to argue with a gun, but he was willing to risk a slap in exchange for information.

"We're going to a place where we can talk in comfort. Now, I don't want to hear any noise. Understand?"

"Understood." He nodded agreement. His brain worked furiously, testing their options. If he and Deirdre showed any resistance, the second man would ride in the back with them to keep them in line. If they appeared thoroughly cowed, there was a good chance that he would succumb to the temptation of a comfortable seat in front. There were no windows through which they could signal for help and the doors locked on the outside.

The driver kept them covered until the second man climbed into the front and twisted in his seat to take over guard duty. Only when they could see nothing but his back did he raise his mask and turn the key in the ignition.

Brian slung his arm around Deirdre's shoulders and pulled her close. She scrunched down behind the shield of his body and, to his annoyance, began to fuss busily with her hair.

They had not been searched. Brian bitterly regretted his refusal to let Deirdre carry her gun. What had she discovered in the cottage bathroom? Did she have it on her or was it still at the cottage? And how the hell could they hope to escape with Dennis a quivering jelly?

The fat man lay on his stomach on the cold steel floor of the van. He couldn't just let him lie there in his condition. He edged away from Deirdre to kneel at his side.

"Get back where you were."

He ignored the command. He was safe until they got wherever they were going for their "talk," and there was some hope in the fact that so far their captors had not revealed their faces.

"Father Duque is not well and he knows nothing about what's going on. He was just doing an old friend a favor."

The hand holding the gun shifted to point at Deirdre. "Do as I say. I won't shoot you yet, but I'm sure you can tell us everything the girl knows, and shooting her wouldn't bother me a bit."

Where were they going? His hope now lay with Dobbs and Ira, but neither of them was really familiar with the terrain. And what about Dennis? He seemed ominously still. If his heart gave way under the strain, it amounted to murder, just as much as if they shot him. He strained to listen above the sound of the rain on the roof and thought he could discern the priest's shallow breathing through the pounding of the blood in his ears.

He tried to peer past the two men in front to get an idea of where they were going. Traffic was light and they were well over the speed limit; highway signs loomed up and disappeared too fast to be read. No welcome siren sounded or flashing lights appeared. A bridge loomed up ahead. They'd been on the road long enough for it to be the bridge across to Fall River.

163

They slowed as they reached the bridge to turn left along the waterfront. He suddenly realized they were on Riverside Avenue in Somerset, the street where Verity Fletcher lived— where, in fact, they were supposed to meet Verity, Caspar, and Susan Meyer at about ten o'clock with a report on the evening's shenanigans. He sneaked a glance at his watch: 9:30. They'd all be sitting around having drinks and wouldn't start to worry for a couple of hours. By then, it might be too late.

Now that they were in familiar territory, he started to recognize landmarks. They passed the power station and then the restaurant where Deirdre and he had eaten. Five minutes farther along on the left stood Verity's house. They were slowing down. Had he been wrong about Verity and Caspar? No. They passed the house and turned into the small shipyard and marina on the right-hand side, where the glare of a black-and-white TV shone from the watchman's shack. Deirdre tensed beside him; maybe this was their chance. The van pulled up by the shack and the window slid open.

"I sure didn't expect no one on a night like this." No hope here. The speaker's voice was slurred by years and drink. The masked man's gun, held low over the backseat, did not waver.

"Good evening, Ben. I know it's a filthy night, but I'm putting her up for the season next week and I couldn't resist a final spin. Here"—the driver's hand flashed out—"have one on me."

"Thank you kindly, sir."

This time, they had been searched and separated. In defiance of his orders, Deirdre had brought her gun. She had been hustled off to the forward cabin of what Brian judged to be a forty-foot sloop. He was shoved into the main cabin along with Dennis, who was lying facedown on one of the bunks, his breath coming in shallow gasps.

"Make yourself at home. I won't bother to tie you up; we have the girl and if you try anything cute, she'll be the one to suffer. Enjoy." The driver of the van had pulled down his mask

164

as soon as they cleared the watchman's hut. The two left, locking the cabin door from the outside.

Brian started to explore. Their captors were chillingly sure of themselves, but he was determined to go down fighting. He found a set of wickedly sharp knives in the galley and helped himself to a couple and to a small cast-iron skillet of skull-crushing heaviness. There was also a bottle of brandy.

He put a hefty slug in a glass. "Dennis, old friend, try some of this. I know you don't usually drink, but it's good for what ails you."

"I'm afraid I'm beyond help," was his despondent reply. Nevertheless, he allowed himself to be eased up on a couple of pillows while he sipped. Gradually, a little color crept back into his gray cheeks.

27

IRA AND DOBBS had managed to track the van until it turned in at the boatyard.

"What do we do now? I'm only a simple veterinarian."

"Call the cops?"

"And what do we tell them? That our friends were caught trespassing on his property by a Bristol householder and that he pulled a gun on them, kidnapped them across the state line, and is probably going to kill them? Somehow, I don't think so."

They sneaked up to the gate in time to hear the exchange with the watchman. Dobbs pressed Ira back farther into the shadows as the van trundled forward to pull up in the shadow of a large yacht already out of the water for the winter. They watched the driver pull a woman's stocking down over his face before he unlocked the rear doors to pull Deirdre, Brian, and Dennis out.

"Follow and try to get the name of the boat," Dobbs whispered. "I'm going to have a word with the watchman."

Dobbs fidgeted in the car. What was keeping Ira? Had he been spotted and shanghaied with the others? He had just decided to investigate when there was a tap on the window.

166

"Forty-foot gaff-rigged sloop, *Copper's Lady,* out of Somerset," Ira reported. "They're headed upstream."

"That checks with what I was able to get out of the watchman, but he's so loaded he'd have agreed chalk was cheese to get the twenty I waved under his nose. I think we should make for Verity's house and bring them up to date. At least there's no longer any doubt about who did it, though I must admit that the second man came as a complete surprise. Representative Meyer will know what our next move should be. What took you so long?"

"I was nosing around the van. I found this in the back." He held out an envelope sealed in heavy plastic.

"What is it?" Dobbs put the car in gear.

"It may be nothing, but it may be what Brian and Deirdre were looking for. Maybe they ditched it when they were caught. We'll take a look when we get to Verity's."

"What's happening?" Verity came rushing out the door, closely followed by Caspar, Representative Meyer, and Rebecca. "Come on in and tell us everything."

Two people rose to their feet as Ira and Dobbs entered the room. Dobbs raised an inquisitive eyebrow at Verity, but it was Representative Meyer who did the honors.

"Professor Dobbs, Dr. Grossman, this is Sergeant Culpepper of the Somerset Police Department and Detective Helga Lindstrom of the attorney general's office. Why don't we have a seat while you tell your story."

28

THE SLOOP'S AUXILIARY motor sprang to life, joining the patter of the rain and the soughing of the wind. Dennis sipped again at his brandy. He touched his chest.

"I think I've had it. The brandy helps, but the old heart is going like blazes."

"Nonsense, we'll get out of this."

"You're whistling in the graveyard. I'm not really afraid. To tell you the truth, it would be a relief."

"I could kick myself for getting you into this."

"Don't. The last few days have been the happiest I've had in years. I wouldn't change a thing."

"Don't talk like that." The boat angled sharply and Brian grabbed the side of the bunk for balance. "It feels like we're turning."

Dennis's eyes were fixed steadily on him. There was an uncomfortable silence before he spoke. "You're an historian. In the Middle Ages many believed that if there was no priest available, any fellow Christian could hear a dying person's confession."

"I've read that, yes. But wasn't it thrown out by the Council of Trent?"

"The hell with the Council of Trent. Old friend, would you hear my confession?"

He felt as if he'd been kicked in the chest. It was the last thing in the world he wanted to do, but what could he say? He knew that Dennis was right. He was dying and every breath was a major triumph of will over his fast-fading life force. He knelt next to the bunk and took Dennis's hands in his own.

"I'd be honored to hear your confession."

"I'm gay, you know."

"I didn't know, but that's no sin."

"I'm not saying it is." He drew a ragged breath. "But it led me into sin." He gripped with manic force. "Sure, there were incidents through the years. Forget them. If God made me this way, I figure He can't blame me. I resolved that side of things a long time ago."

"Then what . . ."

"I love you. I've always loved you. Even when we were little kids at St. Camillus and I didn't know what it was all about. . . . Then we got to be teenagers and I adored you, but you were so goddamn heterosexual that it hurt."

Brian's head reeled. How could he have been so blind? He remembered the shy touches that, in hindsight, were not quite the same as macho horseplay. The way Dennis always went along with what he wanted, would break any date if he beckoned. Still . . .

"But you went out with girls. There were broken hearts from Breezy Point to Far Rock when you left for the seminary."

"I'm talking about fifty years ago. You have no idea what it was like to be gay in the forties. Of course I went out with girls. I thought I was filthy, despicable, and I kept hoping I could cure myself. It's no fun to have people think you're a degenerate. Mother and Dad never guessed, thank God. I knew you had no idea of how I felt.

"I used to daydream of our life together. Sort of a gay *Donna Reed Show* without the kids. I was Donna. I cherished the dream even after I was ordained. Then you came home from the army and got engaged to Maire. My dream died when you asked me to officiate at your wedding."

"I never knew. . . ."

Sweat was running down Dennis's face. "I'm going fast; let

169

me finish. My sin is that I hate Maire. I've never hated anyone the way I hated her on your wedding day. I hated you, too. The two of you were so happy, so sure of yourselves. I let the friendship die, so don't blame yourself. Didn't answer your letters. Didn't call. I was in New York many times but never looked you up.

"I stopped sending Christmas cards. Every birth announcement had me in torment. It was proof that you and she were . . . Oh God." His labored breathing turned into erratic choking gasps. His eyes closed.

Brian sat on the bunk and gathered the priest close in his arms. Dennis's eyes fluttered open and the ghost of a smile crossed his lips. "What was it that Nelson said when he was dying? Show you forgive me."

Brian's arms tightened as the familiar line rose to his lips. " 'Kiss me Hardy, ere my life be spent.' " With a strange mixture of love, repulsion, and pity, he closed his lips gently on those of the dying man. Dennis gave a long sigh and went limp in his arms.

He laid his friend's body down on the bunk, closed his eyes, crossed the still hands on his breast, and covered him with a blanket. There was nothing more to do for him. Mourning could come later, if there was a later. Maybe he'd be reunited with Dennis sooner than he wanted to be.

What was happening to Deirdre? Had they hurt her? They were remarkably sure of themselves to leave him with all the potential weapons a galley affords, or maybe they were just stupid enough to think he'd obey them like a sheep going to market.

Stupid. That was it. Whoever was doing the planning had an inflated sense of his own cleverness combined with a contempt for the rest of humanity. He had come up with this overelaborate scheme to wreck the Delaney Institute, knock off the other heirs, and scoop the pot for himself. Then he couldn't resist making Liza Borden the patsy. Brian was sure that whenever they got where they were going, there would be a falling-out between the two men. It was like a tontine—winner take all. His eyes gleamed. He finally had the full picture. Now, if only he and Deirdre could manage to escape.

He gazed in frustration at the radio set with its missing transmitter. Even if he knew how to use the thing, he couldn't. He flipped a few random switches just in case. The door was solid teak and secured by a stout Chubb lock, the kind reputed to be burglarproof. He considered the portholes and dismissed them—too small to wiggle through even if he managed to unscrew them. He hefted the cast-iron spider thoughtfully; it seemed to be coming down to lurking behind the door and chance his arm on the old blunt instrument.

Maybe the reason they hadn't bothered to tie him and left him with all these potential weapons was that they weren't planning any interrogation at all. Maybe they were just going to sink the boat with the three of them aboard, then escape themselves in the inflatable dinghy he'd seen on the deck and blow up the boat with some sort of explosive device set off by a remote control or a timer. Any way he looked at the situation, he saw nothing but negatives.

If there was some way he could eavesdrop. He pressed his ear to the cabin door but heard nothing. The portholes? Aha! The last one he tried sent back the faint sound of angry voices just tantalizingly beyond clarity. He grabbed a Phillips screwdriver from the tools hanging in neat array on a square of pegboard and attacked the porthole cover, but the screws would not budge. They were corroded in place by exposure to salt air.

What was that trick Dennis had shown him when they were kids and wanted to spy on Brian's elder brother when he took the phone into the hall closet to chat with his girlfriends? A glass tumbler, that was it. Press the hollow end against the door and the other end to your ear and it acted as an amplifier. He grabbed a glass and pressed it against the wall under the porthole. Nothing.

Then he placed it against the glass. Although the sound was flat and tinny, like a crossed telephone connection, he heard them clearly.

"We'll never get away with it."

"Sure we will."

171

"The watchman saw us."

"Ben was drunk and all he saw was your back. And I don't plan to deny that you were aboard. Here's how we'll play it. Just reunited with my long-lost brother . . . tragedy at sea . . . not enough of the body recovered for identification . . . grieving widow. . . . I'll join you as soon as the furor dies down."

"But—"

"No *buts*—it's perfect. We're headed upstream now, so we can anchor and find out what these three clowns know and whom they've told, if anyone. My bet is that we've got all of them and no one else has tumbled to our secret."

"I didn't plan on five murders. . . ."

Brian had heard enough. The bastards were planning to find out how much he and Deirdre knew and who else was in on it, then blow up the boat. He strongly suspected that he would murder his accomplice and send the *Copper's Lady* down to Davy Jones with four bodies instead of three. It was crystal clear that the long-separated O'Connor twins were reunited and as dangerous as a couple of rattlesnakes.

What the hell could he do about it? Certainly he would tell all, make clear that many important and influential people knew everything they had discovered. But would they believe him? He was slumped on the bunk with his head in his hands when the door inched open.

"Deirdre!" She was barefoot and wearing only her bra and panties. She laid a cautionary finger to her lips and motioned for him to flick the curtain across the porthole.

"It's okay; no one can hear us. He's planning to blow up the boat."

"What about Dennis?"

Brian pointed to the shrouded form on the bunk. "Dead."

"We'll have to swim for it; it's our only chance. I'll get the shakes later." She looked down at herself. "You'd better strip."

"No, damn it, I'll freeze."

"You're not the world's greatest swimmer and you'll drown with all those heavy clothes to pull you down. We're not too far from the riverbank if we make our move now. I've been watching out the porthole."

"How did you escape?" He pulled off his sneakers and pants.

"My picklocks. I took the ring apart in the van and hid them in my hair. They weren't too thorough in their search. The locks on this boat are bastards, or I'd have been here sooner."

He pulled off his sweatshirt and stood in undershirt and boxer shorts. Deirdre took a quick look around the cabin.

"Let's see if we can provide a little distraction." She jerked the cover off an electric panel by the sink, grabbed a handful of wires, and pulled. There was a shower of sparks as the power failed and the motor coughed and died.

They stumbled up the few steps to the deck and into the rainy night to the accompaniment of curses and shouts from the two on deck. Dierdre sprang lightly onto the rail and dived cleanly away from the side of the boat. Brian's exit was less aesthetic but equally effective. He scrambled onto the rail, grabbed his nose in one hand, and jumped feetfirst into the water just as a bullet whistled past his nose.

The cold screamed up his legs and belly, then water closed over his head. He fought his way to the surface and found himself to the lee of the sloop, close enough to hide under the curve of the side. There was no sign of Deirdre, but he knew she was a fish in the water. He was worried about himself. His best effort was a slow serviceable breaststroke.

He kicked off, trying to ooze through the water like a seal, fixing his eyes on a friendly light gleaming through the rain. If Deirdre's calculations were correct, he was headed for the Somerset bank of the river and it could only be a matter of minutes before they pursued in the dinghy. He fought down the urge for speed. He knew he couldn't keep up a decent pace against the strong current that plucked at his legs. Then, too close for hope, came the splash as the dinghy hit the water and the steady hum of its outboard motor. He risked a backward glance. The thing was headed straight at him and there

173

was a spotlight mounted on its bow. He took a deep breath and submerged.

His glasses had miraculously remained on his nose when he jumped from the rail, but now they slid off, finding a muddy grave. He started to count. He should be able to stay down at least ninety seconds. He didn't dare try swimming underwater or he'd be completely turned around. One, two, three . . .

Ninety! His lungs bursting, fighting against exhaling, with arms that seemed too weak to stroke, he fought his way to the surface. His stale breath exploded and he gulped in water and air. The dinghy was about fifty yards away, methodically criss-crossing the area between the sloop and the riverbank. It turned and headed back in his direction.

He could no longer spot the light ashore that he had been using as a guide. If only the rain would stop so he could see how far he was from the bank. The spotlight drew closer and he ducked under again to let the boat pass over him. This time, his toe hit against a rock. He inched forward and was re-warded with a definite purchase on the muddy bottom, then took a quick gulp of air and a look before he ducked again. The riverbed shelved upward. Soon he was forced to crawl on all fours, hoping that his head would be mistaken for an exposed rock.

The water dwindled to nothing. He was on the beach. There was a shout and the roar of a motor on full throttle. He had been spotted, and he thought he knew where he was.

He squinted through the rain, cursing his lost glasses. Was that a flight of wooden steps snaking up the bluff that over-looked the beach? There had been stairs like that in the park where Verity and he had disported on the tube slides. Any-way, he had no other choice.

Adrenaline surging, he sprinted for the stairs just as he heard the dinghy grate on the shingle. A shot rang out as he reached the first landing and buried itself in the rail. He kept climbing, weaving from side to side. Now he blessed the steady rain. If he could outdistance the buggers, he had a chance to make it to Verity's house. At least he was off the damn boat. Another bullet whistled past, but his legs could put forth no more speed. The others had been riding around in a boat while he'd been swimming for his life. There was no way he could outdistance them for much longer. He slowed fractionally, ready to give up, when he realized that he was at the top of the stairs and darkness lay ahead.

Deirdre's dive took her well away from the side of the boat and she struck out for the riverbank with strong, sure strokes. She hated leaving her father, but she knew that the best chance for both of them was to get help fast. She lowered her head and streaked through the water. A few minutes later, she waded ashore over slippery rocks, scrambled up the muddy bank through a tangle of weeds and rushes, and took off like a rocket down Riverside Avenue.

A car passed her, stopped, and a man got out into the rain.

"Hey, pretty lady, are you in trouble?" He smacked his lips and spread his arms to intercept her. Scarcely breaking stride, she grabbed one of the outstretched arms and flipped him to the sidewalk.

"Bitch!" he howled at her retreating back.

The boatyard came into view on her left; to her right was Verity's house, shining like a beacon.

She banged on the door. It opened to warmth, refuge, and, above all, help.

29

BRIAN CRAWLED ON hands and knees through a tangle of thorny bushes. He could hear them crashing about, cursing, wondering where he'd disappeared. Now that he had a moment to catch his breath, he took stock of his predicament.

On a physical level, he and his pursuers were pretty much equal—the three of them were about the same age and, he congratulated himself, he was probably in better shape than the others. But there were two of them, fully clothed, less tired, and they had a gun. He didn't doubt at this point that they'd shoot first and ask questions later. Deirdre must have gotten clean away and she'd come back with help. They must realize that by now. All he had to do was play a waiting game. Be sly as a fox, not brave as a lion.

What would a fox do? He'd go to earth, that's what. But where? He couldn't stay where he was for long; they'd be sure to search the thicket in a few minutes. Besides, his legs were quivering; if he stayed still much longer, they'd start to cramp. His best hope was to find a good hiding place and wait for Deirdre to return with the cavalry. She must have reached Verity's by now. Come to think of it, so must have Ira and Dobbs.

He wriggled cautiously to the edge of the briars, wincing

176

when thorns gouged deeper into his already-lacerated back and arms. The two were on the other side of the copse, speaking in low tones. He strained his ears but could only pick up a confused buzz. His hand closed on a stone and he crawled out to fling it as far as he could into the darkness.

There's no trick like an old trick. The shifty duo turned as one and raced toward the sound of the falling rock. Brian stood up as nimbly as his shaking legs allowed and took off farther up the hill.

The wet leaves squelched underfoot, sleeking the rough path. He fell to his knees, arose, and slipped again. The rain was now more a heavy moistness than a true downpour, but that was still enough to obscure the path, even if he'd had his glasses.

He finally reached the brow of the hill and there was his hoped-for objective: the gaping mouth of the orange plastic tube slide that would hurtle him down to land far away from his pursuers and closer to the entrance of the park. He clambered in and blackness folded around him.

He did not push off right away. He surrendered to the illusion of safety. He was so tired and, now that he had a moment to catch his breath, very frightened. The fear was like a thick fog threatening to swirl up and drag him down into a dark pit where evil things lurked. He thought of an old map: Here be monsters.

One of the monsters reached out a tentacle into his mind. You're a stupid old man and they'll catch you. . . . You'll never see Maire again. Maire's face rose up, rosy and comely under the cloud of silver hair. He could hear her voice: Too nosy for your own good . . . and look where it's landed you. He shuddered. What about Deirdre? Was his last sight of her to be a half-clad form jumping into the black waters of a river? And his other children and their children, would they understand? Maybe Verity and Caspar were in league with the men chasing him and Deirdre would walk into a nest of vipers. And Dennis? Dear Dennis, who had loved him for all those years and whom he had led to his death; Dennis, whose final happiness had been a reluctant kiss on his dying lips.

He shook his head violently and crammed the weakening thoughts down to the bottom of his mind. "Quit havering," he murmured, and pushed off down the slide, his scratched back and uncovered legs burning with the friction of his passage. Seconds later, he emerged. They were waiting for him under the playground lights, one on either side.

He looked up at the one with the gun. "Captain McGuire, I expected you, but I admit I was surprised to find out that Leander Seward is your brother."

McGuire gestured with the hand holding the gun. "Get up."

He didn't move. Not because he was brave, but because he feared that his legs would not support him. "How did you get here so quickly?"

"I saw where you were heading and I figured out that you would slide down as soon as you could, so we cut across." He gestured again with the gun. "I saw you and Verity making fools of yourselves on Sunday."

"You followed us?"

"Yeah. You weren't as smart as you thought. I saw you on TV and recognized you right away when you turned up at Delaney pretending to be an out-of-work bum. I've had my eye on you ever since. On your feet."

Keep him talking. "And I thought I fooled everyone."

"I'm a cop with over forty years on the force. It takes more than a beard and dirty clothes to fool me." He turned to Seward, who was hovering in the background. "Lee, go find a rock, a nice big one."

"Why? What do you need a rock for?"

"You don't want to know. Find me the rock, then take a hike for a few minutes."

Brian didn't need anyone to draw him a picture. Guns can be traced; a rock would make a handy puzzle for the Somerset police.

McGuire went on talking in an easy way, as if waiting for Seward and the rock was just a normal social interlude. "Yeah, I followed you on Sunday. I knew you were visiting Liza Borden and I picked you up in Dartmouth as soon as I got out

178

of church. I traded with another lector for an earlier Mass. Quite a day you had."

"What else do you know?"

"I don't know how you dug out so much information on me, and I want to find out. Here comes Lee with the rock. Quit stalling and get up. Or do you want me to use it?"

He rolled over and pushed himself to his hands and knees, then sank back with a groan. "Sorry, I seem to have done something bad to my leg."

Leander Seward stood there with his mouth popping like a fish. He hadn't said a word. Brian shifted his attention to him. "You know, Seward, right now there's not much on you but the business with the bears, and I bet you could get off with a fine and a suspended sentence if you agreed to testify. You must realize that this guy's planning to kill you. He'll bash my brains in, then either shoot you or knock you on the head. He's the one with the gun."

McGuire interrupted. "Shut your face. Lee and I are brothers. He knows I won't hurt him. Why should I?" He laughed. "There's plenty for both of us."

"That's right. Liam and Patrick O'Connor, old Jack Delaney's bastards. How come it took you so long to start nosing around after the Delaney money?"

McGuire roared, "That's enough! On your feet or I swear . . ."

"I told you, I hurt my leg."

"I don't give a damn if you have to walk on your hands; we're going back to the boat."

"So you can blow it up? Lee, myself, and poor Dennis dead of a heart attack brought on by you. Three with one blow."

"Lee, I've had it with this shit. Grab hold of him and help him walk to the dinghy. I'll be right behind you."

"With a gun," Brian muttered urgently as Seward helped him up. "Don't be a fool, man. We've got to work together."

When he put his weight on his right leg, he found he had not been lying. The knee that had plagued him on and off since a football accident in high school had slipped out during his hurtling passage down the slide. Maybe my guardian angel

179

has a plan, he thought. Now I can keep my head close to Seward's ear and plant subversive thoughts.

"He's going to kill both of us. Do you realize that? The man is as crazy as a loon, and if he doesn't kill you, you'll spend the rest of your life in jail. My daughter Deirdre got away, and she's an ex-cop and married to another cop." The arm supporting him twitched convulsively. "The estate is worth about fifty million. Without you, he'll be twice as rich and he'll be rid of a witness."

The arm twitched again. "Shut up!"

"I won't shut up. Why should I? You'll never get away with it, and you're a fool if you trust McGuire." He forgot and put his weight on his bad leg. The pain shot all the way up his side and sweat broke out even though he was shaking with the cold. His teeth clamped down to hold back a scream. What the hell; why shouldn't he scream? He threw back his head and howled like a hyena.

"Quiet," McGuire snarled. He poked the gun hard against Brian's kidneys. "One more yell like that and I'll shoot you here and now."

"You wouldn't dare. Someone might hear the shot and report it. Do you want to explain things to the Somerset cops?"

"I could handle that. I'm a cop too."

"Out of your jurisdiction. They don't like that. There are other people who know about you. You left a trail a mile wide if one knows where to look.

"Keep talking."

He could see the river's edge now and the dark bulk of the dinghy. He had to keep from getting in the boat. Maybe if he offered to tell what he knew . . .

"Look, why don't we sit for a moment? Let me see if I can work my knee back. I've lived with it for so long that I know just what to do. Seward here is about to pass out."

"Keep moving. We're almost there."

A vast weariness swept over him. Suddenly, all he cared about was resting. As they approached a large flat rock, he twisted out of Seward's grasp and flung himself down. He stretched out his right leg and grasped above and below the knee to give a familiar twist. His knee popped back.

"Give it up, man. If I was the only one who knew, there'd be some sense to what you're doing. But Dobbs knows, my daughter Deirdre knows, Dr. Grossman knows, and Verity and Caspar know, to say nothing of Representative Meyer and the attorney general. In other words, your goose is well and truly cooked." Brian had gone too far. McGuire raised the gun, took aim, then thought better of it and brought the butt smashing down on Brian's head.

It could not have been too hard a blow. When he came to, he was in the bottom of the dinghy, trussed like the Christmas goose with which he had just compared McGuire. Better not to let them know he was awake. Their backs were to him as they bent to the oars. Very wise of them to row; the roar of the outboard might catch someone's attention. McGuire was soothing Seward with phony Irish charm.

"Be logical for a moment. Why would I want to hurt you? I've only just found my twin brother, and he's a man of character and education—went to Yale University, no less. There's more than enough for two in our father's estate. And he'd have wanted us to have it, not waste it on a bunch of animals. After all, we're of the same blood. And it's blood that counts."

"But, he said . . ."

"I'm a rough man who hasn't had your advantages and I sometimes say things in the heat of the moment that I don't mean. When this is all over, we'll look back on this night and have a good laugh together. Look at it this way—we're entitled. That Abby Meyer was a nosy bitch and not really one of our kind; she only got what she deserved. The same for Dennis Duque and Sean O'Connor. Priest or no priest, Dennis was gay, for God's sake. And Sean was a disgrace with his long hair and hippie lifestyle."

"I never thought it would go this far. When we first planned it, you didn't say anything about all these murders."

"But there's no real evidence. There's nothing to connect

either one of us with Abby Meyer's death. Sean died in a tragic fire set by a nut. Nothing to connect us to it and it shouldn't be too hard to arrange an accident for his kids. Dennis Duque had a heart attack—natural causes. When all this is settled, you'll be able to start your own college, if that's what you want."

"But what about that girl who escaped and all the other people he says know everything?"

"Are we rowing round in circles? It's taking a hell of a long time to reach the boat. I checked up on Donodio. He's some kind of a nut about police work. Meddled in a case last summer with the NYPD. Poor man's Sherlock Holmes. Wants all the credit. I doubt if he's told anyone but the girl what he's found out. If we take care of her, we'll be home free."

The dinghy bumped gently against the side of the *Copper's Lady*. Brian decided it was time to wake up. He had no intention of being dragged aboard like a sack of potatoes. He groaned and opened his eyes.

McGuire shone his flashlight, dazzling him. "I'm going to untie you so you can climb aboard. I don't want any funny business, or you'll get a bullet through your back. Understand?"

He nodded. Deirdre, where are you?

"Good." He felt the coolness of a blade slip between his wrists and ankles.

"Lee, I want you to go aboard first, then Donodio. I'll bring up the rear."

"That way, you'll have us both covered. How handy."

"Shut up, unless you want to be covered in a way you won't like."

His feet were bleeding from the rocks. His knee protested the insults that had been heaped upon it and sent stabbing pains up to his groin. His undershirt was in shreds over his lacerated back, his soaked boxer shorts made a travesty of modesty, and everything was reduced to fuzzy outlines by the loss of his bifocals, but his hands and feet were free. He gripped the sides of the short ladder to climb to the deck. He'd be damned if he was going down without a fight.

182

His foot hit the deck and Seward made a grab for him. Brian backhanded him across the mouth and turned just as McGuire's head appeared above the railing, one hand holding the gun, the other on the side of the ladder. Now! He grabbed the railings with both hands, lowered his head, and butted McGuire square in the middle of the chest, on the sternum.

McGuire's finger closed convulsively on the trigger as he slipped backward off the ladder, landing on his head with a sickening crunching sound in the bottom of the dinghy. The bullet clipped the edge of Brian's ear and traveled on, burying itself in Leander Seward's chest.

He stood for a moment, not feeling the pain, fatigue, or cold, and then he started to shake. His stomach revolted, spewing up yellow-green bile that burned his throat and rose into his nose so that he had to fight for breath. The last thing he saw was the cold, wet deck rising up to meet him.

Five minutes later, there was the hum of an engine and a spotlight shone on the *Copper's Lady*. A voice came through the bullhorn. "This is the Somerset Police."

30

SMELL WAS THE first of his senses to return. It sent messages to his brain, but he was too groggy to interpret them: something antiseptic and medicinal mixed with something familiar, something he liked. It meant home and safety and love. He breathed in again, trying to force his unwilling mind to connect the separate clues.

No good. He was much too tired. He plunged back into the welcoming darkness where he didn't have to deal with anything.

Hours later, he surfaced again. This time, there was no problem. His nose told him that he was in a hospital and that Maire was with him. Maire! My God, I was supposed to meet her flight at La Guardia on Thursday. How long have I been here? He opened his eyes.

He was cranked up in a hospital bed to a semisitting position. Oxygen tubing was clipped to his nose and two IV stands, one feeding into his arm and the other into his ankle, were dripping merrily. By the feel of it, there was also a catheter emptying discreetly into a bag beneath the bed. He turned his head in the direction of the mingled scents of castile soap, lavender water, and herbal shampoo that spelled Maire and was rewarded with a sickening stab of head pain that almost sent him spinning back into oblivion.

"Maire?"

A hand covered his with a tenderness that belied the dryness of her voice. "Who else, you idiot?"

"What day is it?"

"It's Wednesday night. You've been out of it for nearly twenty-four hours."

"How did you get here? You're not supposed to be here until tomorrow."

"Deirdre called me and I flew into Providence." She squeezed his hand. "That's enough talk for now. I have to call the nurse and tell her you're awake." She pushed the buzzer.

"Wait. Before the medical herd stampedes in, tell me what happened. How's Deirdre?"

"She's fine. Con's furious. McGuire has a broken neck and is paralyzed. Leander Seward had surgery for a bullet in the chest and is recovering in the ICU."

"What about Liza?"

"She was released this morning and the cops have been waiting for you to regain consciousness so they can get your statement. Satisfied?"

"Not really. When can I get out of here? And where am I?"

They were interrupted by a no-nonsense middle-aged nurse who was firm in her allegiance to starched uniforms, white stockings, and a black-banded cap skewered with a hat pin to her coronet of graying braids. She was probably the vanguard of the medical invasion.

"Well, Dr. Donodio, it's nice to have you back with us." She fixed Maire with a beady eye. "We'll have to ask you to step outside for a few minutes while Doctor is with the patient."

Maire was made of stern stuff. She stood her ground, or, to be more precise, sat her seat. "We would like a word with Doctor. We think *we'll* just wait."

"We can't do that. We think Doctor will be glad to see you outside."

185

"Well, *we* think Doctor will just have to lump it."

"It's all right, nurse," Brian's tone was pacific. "Both Mrs. Donodio and I would rather see him together."

"Her."

"I beg your pardon?"

"Dr. McGowan is a lady doctor."

"All the more reason—" His reply was cut off by the entrance of Dr. McGowan, an attractive woman in her mid-thirties with dark hair and brown eyes. She radiated good health and energy.

"I'm Mary McGowan, and you're the hero of the hour. How are you feeling?"

"All the better for seeing you. I was expecting a procession of lumpy interns. This is my wife, Maire Donodio."

"I've been hoping to have a word with you, Mrs. Donodio. I kept missing you earlier." The nurse gave an outraged sniff. "I can manage here, Nurse. Thanks for paging me." Her fingers closed over Brian's wrist. "How's the head?"

"Not bad. Painful when I move it."

She shot a beam into his eyes. "Hmmm. Well, that's to be expected. You were concussed when they brought you in. How much do you remember?"

"The last thing I remember is sitting on a rock and snapping my knee back into place."

"Well, I understand that a lot happened after that. It may come back to you, or you may never regain the memory. Head trauma is a funny thing." She checked his chart. "I think you can get rid of the IVs and the catheter and I'll order something for the pain if you need it. Are you hungry?"

He suddenly realized that he was ravenous. "I'll say."

"An excellent sign. I'll have the kitchen send something up. Mrs. Donodio, if he keeps this up, he can leave the hospital tomorrow. I want you to make sure that his doctor in New York gives him a thorough checkup." She folded up her stethoscope and jammed it in her pocket.

"Not so fast, young lady. I have a few questions before you leave."

"Fire away."

186

"First. What hospital is this?"

"That's easy. St. Anne's in Fall River."

"Next, what's the matter with me?"

"Most men your age would be basket cases after all you went through, but you're a tough old bird."

"Thanks, I think, for the compliment—if it is one. I meant specifically."

"Concussion, hypothermia, exposure, exhaustion, and superficial abrasions. We were afraid you might develop pneumonia, but that complication seems remote. The jury is still out on what you may have absorbed from drinking the Taunton River; that's why you've been getting intravenous antibiotics as a precaution."

"Maire tells me that Bill McGuire has a broken neck and Leander Seward is in the ICU. What happened to them?"

"They're both at Charlton Memorial Hospital, so I wouldn't know. I understand that the police thought it better to have you in a different hospital. I know the cops have been anxious to get your statement. Shall I tell them that you feel up to it? I'll allow them to stay for only ten minutes but"—there was a portentous pause—"you'll have to speak with them before your press conference."

"Press conference?" Brian and Maire spoke as one.

Dr. McGowan's eyes danced with glee. "The media people are camped out in the lobby. You don't seem to realize that you're the biggest sensation to hit this town since the first Lizzie Borden trial. You solved the case. You got Liza out of jail. There's a dead priest, a crooked cop, and a crazy college president. Then, to cap the climax, all sorts of revelations about Jack Delaney, to say nothing of your finding the stolen bears. Of course there's going to be a press conference. You're a hero."

Brian's and Maire's eyes met. Brian winked. "It sure as hell beats bus trips to Atlantic City from a senior citizens' center."

31

Two weeks later, Brian and Maire were on the way to New Haven, where everyone concerned in Liza Borden's vindication was meeting at Philander Dobbs's house. Maire was driving.

"Oh no you don't," she'd exclaimed when he tried to beat her to the driver's seat. "I'd be a nervous wreck and arrive at Phil's house with a splitting headache. I'm driving."

"I managed when you were in Kansas City," he protested mildly.

"That's not the point. You refused to drive for so many years that it makes me uneasy to see you behind the wheel."

The traffic was brutal leaving New York. Despite new prowess at the wheel, he gladly surrendered to the pleasures of the passenger seat and a chance to mull over once again the events of the last couple of weeks.

The police had taken his statement while he was still in St. Anne's and he had managed, to Deirdre's relief, not to reveal Con's involvement. Then came the three-ring press conference on a hastily improvised stage in the lobby of the hospital.

The media was there in a shouting, jostling crowd: NBC, CNN, CBS, ABC, PBS, CBC, TNT, the BBC, AP, UPI—a veritable alphabet soup—as well as *Time, U.S. News & World Re-*

port, Newsweek, The New York Times, the *Boston Globe,* and others too numerous to mention.

Everyone wanted to get in on the act. Representative Meyer lined up with Abby's father, Bernard Meyer. The Globe Street Irregulars were out in force. So were Sergeant Culpepper of the Somerset police and Detective Lindstrom of the attorney general's office, each anxious to have a little of Brian's glory to burnish their shields. Verity and Caspar lent dignity. Brian was trying, with his bandaged head, to project a becomingly modest and frail persona when he was abruptly upstaged by the entrance of Rebecca Betancourt Delgado, Esq., the darling of the media, who preceded Liza and Joshua to the platform.

Liza looked as if a careless puff of wind could flatten her. Her hands shook and her bloodless lips trembled. She leaned on Joshua for support and he kept a steadying arm about her waist as she read from a prepared statement.

"Ladies and gentlemen, my heart is too full of conflicting emotions to be able to discuss——"

She was interrupted by cries of "Louder. We can't hear you. Use the mike. . . ."

A little hectic color rose in her cheeks and her hands quivered so violently that she could not read her statement. She gulped to hold back her tears. Rebecca helped her to a seat and grabbed the mike.

"My client is in no shape to face a crowd after her false arrest and unjust imprisonment, but she insisted on coming today to express her gratitude publicly to all the friends who rallied to her cause—particularly Dr. Brian Donodio and his daughter, Deirdre, who believed in her innocence and laid their lives on the line to prove it.

"Ladies and gentlemen, it is my pleasure and honor to give tribute to and present to you the man of the hour, Dr. Brian MacMorrough Donodio."

Dobbs muttered out of the corner of his mouth, "If that one isn't running for public office within the year, I'll eat my hat. Get up to the mike; they're waiting for you."

Oh joy, oh bliss, oh perfect fulfillment of boyhood fantasy.

189

All that was lacking was a tucket of trumpets and a roll of drums somewhere in the distance. He hadn't had this much fun in years. He arranged his features to becoming modesty and stepped forward.

"I am just pleased that my colleagues"—he gestured to the assembled group—"and I have been able to serve the cause of justice. My pleasure is, alas, tempered with sadness. I never knew Abby Meyer, but my heart and sympathy go out to her family." He bowed to Bernard Meyer and Representative Meyer. "I am also saddened by the death of my boyhood friend, Father Dennis Duque. He was a good man and the beloved pastor of St. Fiacre's Parish. May he rest in peace." He held up his hand. "I'm sorry neither I nor my colleagues are able to answer specific questions at this time. The police and our brilliant counsel, Ms. Betancourt Delgado, do not wish us to say anything that may prove prejudicial to the case against Bill McGuire and Leander Seward. Thank you."

Amid the shouts and grumbles of the frustrated reporters, the police led them out the back door and into the hospital parking lot.

The house in Woodside had seemed an oasis of peace. The peace lasted for about fifteen minutes, then the first of the phone calls came. It was *People* magazine wanting to interview him.

He agreed. He agreed also to an article in *The New York Times Magazine*. A scheme was building in his mind, an idea of a proper occupation for his golden years. He almost changed his mind when he saw the cover of *People*.

AMERICA'S WIMSEY: DONODIO VIEWS THE BODY the headline screamed in Bodoni Ultra type over his picture.

The *Times* was more circumspect. Its article inquired: "The return of the amateur sleuth? In the tradition of Dorothy L. Sayers's Peter Wimsey, Charlotte MacLeod's Peter Shandy, and Jane Langton's Homer Kelly, real-life amateur sleuth Brian Donodio is building a reputation as a man who gets results. . . ."

190

Then there had been Dennis's internment at the Sulpician Motherhouse after the Requiem Mass at St. Fiacre. He and Maire had been joined by Finbar in the little chapel and followed the simple pine box to its resting place under a maple still clothed in its red-gold glory.

He lingered at the graveside. Before the coffin was covered, he poured sand from Rockaway Beach and earth from the shores of Jamaica Bay into the grave.

He bowed his head. Rest in peace, dear friend. I wish I had known how you felt, not that I could have done anything about it. As it is, I'll take your secret to my own grave.

Brian glanced up to see how far they'd come. Maire was negotiating the turn off the turnpike into New Haven. Not far now. He closed his eyes again.

One thing still bothered him, one loose end. He hated loose ends and he knew that this one could never be tied up to his satisfaction; he could only speculate. He hadn't proved that Detective Suarez was the one blackmailing Dennis, though he was fairly sure. When he tried to find out, Dennis had invoked the seal of confession and there was no more to be said.

Suarez was a single man in his thirties. Maybe he, too, was gay. He might have seen Dennis in a gay hangout—not in Fall River, of course; possibly in Boston, New York, or Toronto—and recognized him. His next move was to make a phony confession of his own preference and make sure Dennis knew who he was. Then he could blackmail him with impunity, knowing that Dennis could do nothing about it without breaking the seal. It was a neat solution, but was it the true one? He'd never know, but he'd bet his shirt on it if he was a betting man.

The car stopped. He opened his eyes. They were outside Dobbs's house.

"Is this the right place? Why didn't you tell me?"

"Because I wanted to see your face when you saw it."

"Robert Mills?"

191

He chuckled. "You've got it in one. Come on, my dear. We mustn't keep our host waiting."

"Why would anyone want to live in a little copy of the Treasury Building?"

"You'd have to ask Dobbs's ancestors, and they're in no position to talk." He led her up the marble steps and rang the bell.

Dobbs opened the door. "You two are the last to arrive. Con and Deirdre are here and so are the Fall River contingent and Ira."

He led them through to the sunroom, where Liza sat enthroned in a peacock chair, with Joshua hovering protectively. Deirdre and Con were off in a corner engaged in a muttered discussion. By the set of Deirdre's jaw and the redness of Con's face, trouble seemed to be brewing.

The Globe Street Irregulars were gathered around the bar with Verity, Caspar, and Rebecca, busily bending their elbows. José and Rosa sat on the couch, looking a little bemused but happy. Only Representative Meyer was missing.

"Where's Susan Meyer?"

"We invited her, but she said that she just couldn't face a gathering where everyone will be talking about Abby. Of course I told her we understood." Dobbs answered.

When Brian and Maire appeared in the doorway, a chorus went up from the assembled company:

See the conquering hero comes!
Sound the trumpets, beat the drums!

They howled in an off-pitch rendition that would have pained poor old Handel.

Emily set a chair in the middle of the floor for Brian and pressed a glass into his hand. He sniffed and his eyebrows rose. "Glenties single malt. Dobbs, I'm overwhelmed."

"It seemed the least we could do, knowing your preference. I had a hard time finding it in New Haven, but I persevered. I'm developing quite a taste for it.

192

"Now, tell all. All of us have questions. Mine is, how did you figure out that Bill McGuire was the evil genius?"

"Was? Didn't he make it?"

"He'll be able to stand trial, but he's paralyzed. I meant *was* in the sense that his fangs have been pulled."

"What about Seward?"

"I hear he's singing like a birdie," Finbar offered. "It will all come out at the trial when he testifies."

"Well"—Brian looked around—"you all had vital parts to play and this is my reconstruction. It may be wrong as to details.

"The first thing that struck me was that no one seemed to have any obvious personal motive for killing Abby. That meant that her death had to be part of a larger scheme. It was when Sean told me that she was a granddaughter of old Delaney that the penny dropped. Framing Liza was an overelaborate embroidery based on the Borden name."

Joshua ran a loving hand over Liza's head. Her hair had regained its bounce and shine, but the gray streaks gave mute testimony to her ordeal. "We've decided to change our name back to Brodsky legally. Rebecca is making the arrangements."

"Good decision." André applauded.

"What about the bears, the eagle chicks, and the other animals?" Ira asked.

"The bears may have started out as an unrelated issue brought about by Seward's obsession with his masculine function, or McGuire may have played on the man's sexual inadequacy and put him up to the bear caper in order to have him under his thumb. He may even have helped him find the talent for the snatch. What we found out from José's foraging through the data banks was that they were stolen right after the time that both Seward's adoptive mother and McGuire's adoptive father died.

"I can't be sure, but this was probably when they found out their real identities from the family papers."

Finbar nodded. "I think you're right. I remember when Seward's mother died; that's when he went off half-cocked. It must have been an awful blow to discover that he was not a Mayflower type but the illegitimate son of an Irishman, no matter how rich, and a Bedford Street lady."

"Whereas McGuire didn't give a damn; all he cared about was the chance to get his hands on fifty million. In order to do that, he had to get rid of all the direct descendants and put Delaney out of business. The bears served a double purpose—they gave him a hold over Seward and they started the demise of the institute. The key to the whole case lay in Mrs. Delaney's will."

Con was listening intently. "How did he find out that Seward was his twin?"

José answered. "Probably the same way I did—tapped into the data banks. His adoption papers or old correspondence with Delaney's lawyers may have revealed that he was a twin. There was probably material pertaining to the trust fund. He must have wondered about his missing brother and checked to see if there was another fund set up at the same time in the same bank. Maybe all he had to do was have a quiet word with a bank officer. After all, he was a police captain and head of the Major Crime Unit."

"Then," Deirdre added, "it was easy to track Seward down and find out that he was corruptible. I guess they were twins in everything."

"Fifty million dollars is a powerful motive," Caspar observed, "and he was in a perfect position to sabotage the institute. When were you sure?"

Brian tapped his nose. "I got suspicious when I found out that he refused to connect the investigation into the sabotage at Delaney with the murder investigation, insisting they were two separate cases. After he killed Abby and lured Liza to North Park, he placed the call to the police himself. Rebecca got a copy of the tape, and while the voice cannot be identified, it's clearly disguised. But, to answer your question, Caspar, I wasn't absolutely certain until Deirdre, Dennis, and I were hijacked in Bristol."

"What made you so sure at that point?"

"They were both masked, but I could smell a trace of my

favorite whiskey"—he raised his empty glass and Dobbs hurried to refill it—"on one of them. When I first met McGuire, I thought maybe I had misjudged him, because he smelled of Glenties single malt. At that time, I didn't suspect him of anything worse than stupidity."

Con waved his hand for attention. "What about Umberto Suarez? How is he connected? I hate to see him get away with blackmail. And what was he blackmailing Dennis about?"

Brian had hoped this question would not arise. "With Dennis dead, I doubt if we'll ever know for sure. I did have a word with Susan Meyer, who promised to whisper in various ears. I think Detective Suarez is going to find himself the object of some unwelcome official attention in the near future."

"But . . ."

"Con, let a man take his secrets to the grave. If Suarez was the one blackmailing Dennis, I'm sure he has other victims on the hook, as well."

Liza stood up. "Dr. Donodio . . ."

"Please, call me Brian."

"Brian, Joshua and I owe you something that can never be repaid but"—she handed him a small gift-wrapped package—"please accept this as a remembrance of a time I'd rather forget."

Brian loved presents, the anticipating, poking, speculating. He ran his hands over the little package. Could it be? He loosened the wrapping and extracted a small faded green volume. The 1855 edition of *Leaves of Grass,* signed. Whitman himself had touched this book.

"I'm overwhelmed. I don't know what to say. This should be in one of the great libraries." He turned to Maire with shining eyes. "We'll have to get a special case built for it."

Dobbs broke the mood. "Let's drink to Whitman."

But it was Ira who had the last word. "The bears. How in hell did Seward steal three bears and get them into that obscene little hut?"

"I don't know, Ira. Maybe he hired Goldilocks to tell them their new house in the woods was ready."

EPILOGUE

CON AND DEIRDRE lay rigidly side by side, the argument that festered between them putting a damper on gentler pleasures.

"I think it's a lousy idea." Con spoke through clenched teeth. "I don't want you to be a rotten private investigator."

"What about what *I* want?"

"You're my wife," he answered, as though there was no more to be said.

"But not your slave, or your property. You know I have to work. You can't expect me to spend all my time rotting away here in the house."

"Why not? My mother did it and she didn't 'rot away.'"

"In case you haven't noticed, I'm not your mother!"

"You could always have a baby."

She reared up on her elbow and practically hissed into his face. "I can't believe what I'm hearing. You want us to have a child so I won't be bored, so I'll have an 'occupation'? I expected something better from you!"

"I thought you wanted children."

"I do. But for the right reasons."

Con was backpedaling fast. "Well, I only thought that now would be the perfect time. You're out of work. You could take the next police exam; it will be a couple of years before your name comes up on the list for appointment."

"Have you been discussing this with my father?"

"As God is my judge . . ."

"Okay, I believe you. I haven't discussed it with him either, but from something he said this afternoon, I think he might like the idea. I should have no trouble getting a license."

"Why can't you get a regular job? You could teach or be a social worker or——"

She interrupted. "I want to be a cop and this is a good way to mark time." Her fingers brushed against his arm.

He remembered a talk he'd had with Brian when Deirdre and he got engaged. Brian had said, "Just as long as you know she's an adult and treat her like one, it will all work out." Then he thought of Deirdre and all the other police wives, husbands, and parents who lived with daily fear. Who was he to deny her the choice he had made himself? His hand reached out.

In Woodside, Brian and Maire were getting ready for bed. He hopped in first and patted her side invitingly.

"What a glorious day. Come here, my love, my dove, my fair one."

Maire put her glasses on the bedside table, slid her feet out of her fuzzy slippers, and snuggled comfortably into the crook of his arm. "I have one question before we settle down to the important business of the evening."

"Ask away, my dear. I know you're as nosy as I am."

"I thought it might be indelicate to bring this up at your party. Tell me, did you finally realize that Dennis was gay and had a thing for you years ago?"

My God! He'd always suspected Maire was a witch. "What ever gave you such an idea? Why, when he went away to the seminary there were broken hearts all over New York."

She drew a satisfied breath. "I thought so. I won't mention it again. Now, what is it that you've been saving up to tell me?"

"I've made a decision, but I have to speak with Deirdre. I think I'm developing a knack for investigation."

"You've been lucky twice."

"But I shall hone my skills and take no more silly risks. Deirdre needs a job. I shall give her one as my partner. Dono-dio et Filia, Inc. How does that sound? She can get the license and I'll bill myself as a consultant."

"Con will have a fit."

"If Deirdre is agreeable, Con will have to lump it. She's her mother's daughter."

"And her father's. Con might as well find out early what he's taken on." She moved in the pattern of maximum delight, and all the world was skin.